Books by Sally M. Russell:

An Escape For Joanna
*Finding A Path To Happiness
*Dr. Wilder's Only True Love

*Haven of Rest Ranch Series

DR. WILDER'S ONLY
TRUE LOVE

Sally M. Russell

authorHOUSE®

AuthorHouse™
1663 Liberty Drive
Bloomington, IN 47403
www.authorhouse.com
Phone: 1-800-839-8640

First published by AuthorHouse 2/21/2011

ISBN: 978-1-4567-4497-7 (e)
ISBN: 978-1-4567-4496-0 (sc)

Library of Congress Control Number: 2011902859

Printed in the United States of America

*Any people depicted in stock imagery provided by Thinkstock are models,
and such images are being used for illustrative purposes only.
Certain stock imagery © Thinkstock.*

This book is printed on acid-free paper.

To Henry,

Even though I knew very little about the life of a doctor, getting to know you over the years most likely inspired me to base the main character of this book in the unusual role of a heart specialist and also a general surgeon. Having a young man from a previous book become a patient in the hospital, it was only natural to pick the unmarried doctor to be the object of another romantic involvement.

Dr. Henry Russell was a surgeon for several years before becoming a medical director and patient safety consultant. I want to thank him for the great help he's so freely given to me when I've asked, not only for this book but for at least two of my later books.

When Dr. Wilder reached the door to Josh's room, he heard the most captivating voice. He saw Liz sitting in a chair, but his eyes were drawn to the nurse standing beside the bed talking to Josh. She was tall, about 5'8" he would guess, a beautiful woman with long brunette hair falling to her shoulders. When he'd first seen her, his heart had started beating like a young lion on its first hunt, but with his luck, could he possibly help her solve the dilemma she faces?

All the days ordained were written in your book before one of them came to be. Psalm 139:16

CHAPTER ONE

Dr. Dan Wilder couldn't get his mind off the events of the afternoon even though he'd finally stretched out in his big comfortable recliner with the day's newspaper spread across his chest. He'd worked Saturday and Sunday so had decided to take Monday off and drive down to Hayes to see what his cousin, Tim, was doing on the Fourth of July. He had hoped to talk him into going to the Haven of Rest Ranch, where they might've been able to rent a couple of horses to see if he could actually stay on one. After all the years of dreaming about the thrill of riding, however, he was again disappointed that it hadn't happened. His bad luck with animals just seems to continue.

He'd gone to lunch with Tim and his girlfriend, Kate, which was fine, but Tim had been on duty with the Fire and Rescue Squad over the holiday weekend. So, when he and his partner received an emergency call, Dan had decided to just leisurely drive back to Colorado Springs.

He'd actually driven over to the scenic road that would take him the long way back home.

He hadn't been on this road for years, and he could see that a lot of changes had taken place. The trees along the newly resurfaced road had grown to be quite large which gave a nice ethereal feeling to the drive. When he glanced over to the area where he and Tim used to go fishing, he was amazed that the copse that had been there at that time was now a fairly thick forest. He decided to venture in and see what the lake looked like after all these years, but as he got closer it didn't look at all like it had when he was a kid. It appeared more like a private club than the little farm he remembered. He was stopped at an entrance which had a guard house and two hefty men on duty. "Hello, may we help you?" one of the men asked.

"I'm afraid I may be intruding on private property. My cousin and I used to come out here and fish, but that was quite a few years ago. I see it has changed considerably. I'm Dan Wilder from Colorado Springs, but I was raised in the little town of Hayes back there a few miles."

"Dr. Dan Wilder?" the other asked. "I remember that your dad was the dentist there for years, and you're known as the best heart specialist around. Would you like to take a drive around to see what has been done with the lake? The area was donated to the county when the owner died about five years ago. It's a public recreational area, but you have to get an entrance card yearly from the county. They're hoping that will hold down on some of the misuse and vandalism that is so common these days.

The lake has been enlarged and a nice beach was created on the east side. Paddle boats were purchased so people can rent them by the hour, and if they want, they can watch players on two fairways and greens that can be seen from the lake. An 18-hole golf course was constructed to the west of the lake, which becomes a big hazard as it extends along the side of the two fairways with their bunkers and trees. It then makes a bend to create another tricky water hazard on another fairway before you reach its green.

A large club house was built which has an indoor and outdoor swimming pool, a rather fancy dining room, a game room, and also a room that can be reserved for private or community special events. They've been planning a ballpark to the north, along with a picnic area and playground, but I think that's in next year's budget."

"Are you sure it would be all right for me to drive around? I won't stay long because I really need to be getting back to the hospital."

"Just keep on the road that goes by the club house and you'll find a road taking off to the south that leads to the lake and golf course. Enjoy your visit and maybe you'll even want to get a yearly pass and take advantage of the club someday," he'd chuckled.

Dan had enjoyed seeing what a little country lake could develop into, but a little while later, when he'd almost reached his apartment, he'd gotten a call from his cousin, Tim. He'd been told that they had just delivered a young man, by the name of Josh Holcomb, to the ER. He'd apparently been thrown from the horse he'd been riding at the Haven of Rest Ranch this afternoon. There was definitely a broken arm, but also possible internal injuries. He had still been unconscious upon arrival and was having x-rays taken right then.

Even though he had the day off, Dan had known he'd respond when Tim casually mentioned that this Josh Holcomb was the brother of Christy Hayes' new boyfriend--maybe even her fiancé. As one of the head surgeons, he'd had to be sure that all went well for this young man.

It's that beautiful young woman, Christy Hayes, with the blonde hair and those bright blue eyes, however, who had arrived at the hospital with other members of the family, that now has his thoughts going back ten or more years to when he was growing up in Hayes. His father had been the only dentist, and Dan had grown up in one of the larger homes at the edge of town with enough acreage to be a small ranch. He'd always wanted a pet, but without so much as an explanation, his dad had refused his requests for an animal, especially the horse he'd always dreamed of owning.

Consequently, he'd grown up thinking that his dad must really detest animals, and he was making him suffer because of it. He'd even thought maybe his dad hated him, too, since he'd spent more time with his nanny than he had with his parents.

To compensate for not having a horse of his own, he had gone to the Haven of Rest Ranch, whenever they were holding competitions or a show day, and watched the lucky kids who could own, or at least rent, a horse to ride. While he was in high school, he'd played on the basketball and track teams, but he would still find time to go to the Ranch to watch the horses being put through their paces. Away from school, he'd spent most of his time alone except when he and Tim had planned something together like the fishing at the lake.

Following his college pre-med classes and before entering medical school, he'd gone home for the summer, went to the Ranch quite often and was captivated by a very cute blue-eyed blonde, only 12 or 13 years old. She rode a yearling they'd announced as Rainbow, and the rider was Christy Hayes. She was an expert rider, and he couldn't take his eyes off her. All that summer, he'd watched almost every event held at the Ranch and fell hopelessly in love, from afar of course, with Christy Hayes. He couldn't understand his feelings for a little girl at least ten years his junior, but she was in his dreams almost every night.

That fall he'd left for the long, exciting but stressful, years of medical school, then intern and residency commitments, and finally started his practice in Colorado Springs three years ago.

He hadn't forgotten Christy Hayes, though, and he still spends a lot of time alone and dreaming. *Why am I so tied up in knots after seeing her today at the hospital? She could be engaged to be married, I understand, so why can't I just let it go? I almost made a complete fool of myself when she came into the waiting room this afternoon. I'd just finished talking to Josh's parents about the diagnosis, but if I hadn't left when I did, I don't know what I might have said to her.*

Dropping the paper on the coffee table, he got up and ambled to the tiny kitchen in the apartment he had leased, which was only about five blocks from the hospital. He was looking for something to drink because his mouth was dry, and he felt as if he'd lost one of his most treasured possessions. "Christy Hayes was never mine to have or to lose, and she never will be," he almost screamed at himself as he grabbed a soda from the refrigerator. "I just hope she isn't at the hospital when I make my rounds tomorrow."

❧

The next morning, when Dan stepped quietly into Josh's room, luckily Christy was not there. The pretty little blonde, with the extraordinary brown eyes, who had been with the family in the waiting room yesterday, was standing beside the bed, however. She was talking so very softly to Josh, but Dan could still hear most of her words as he approached the other side of the bed and waited for her to acknowledge his presence.

"I'm not a fairy princess, Josh," she'd whispered, "but maybe I could pretend and we could see if my kiss would do some wake-up magic like in those fairy tales."

Dan certainly hadn't meant to intrude on her conversation, but he could tell she was a little embarrassed when she'd looked up and realized he'd come into the room. She hadn't been afraid to put him in his place later, however, when he'd asked a rather personal question about Christy's fiancé.

"Your patient is Josh, Dr. Wilder, not Jon," she'd informed him quite sternly, and he'd had to ask her name again since he couldn't remember a word Christy had said when she was introducing the ones with her yesterday. She'd then replied, "I'm Liz Becker, Dr. Becker's daughter, and I've been praying so hard that there'd be a better report on Josh's condition by the time you made your rounds today. Will you be able to tell if he'll wake up soon?"

He knew Dr. Becker, a pediatrician at the hospital, and he remembered seeing Liz visiting from time to time with some of the older patients. He'd guess her to be about 15 or 16 years old, and he knew very few teens that young who would be willing to do what she does by giving time to those who are lonely. Many of the older patients have so very few visitors and are really thankful for anyone who will spend time with them. He had surely been impressed. Of course, his curiosity is really aroused now after hearing this sweet sentiment being expressed to his patient. *What is their relationship?* he wondered.

Dan took the chart and studied it for a minute or two, then went over to the bed to check Josh's arm as well as his eyes, ribs and head. The x-rays and Cat Scan that had been taken yesterday had shown no internal organ damage, but there were a few bruised ribs and a big swollen lump on his head. He finally remarked, "Well, Liz, everything looks about the same, and it's difficult to predict when he'll respond. I'll order the IV to be continued, and I'll be back in a little while to see if there's any change. Maybe a fairy princess *will* visit him in the meantime and get him to wake up." He'd even given her an encouraging smile as he started toward the door.

❧

It wasn't too long after lunch when Dr. Wilder was notified that Josh had awoke quite unexpectedly. The doctor was really smiling as he headed for his patient's room. *Did the fairy princess actually kiss him and wake him up?* he pondered as he approached the side of Josh's bed. It was amazing to see Josh so alert, as if he really could have been awakened by the magic kiss of a princess. He tried very hard to suppress a chuckle after he'd quickly glanced at Liz and noticed that she was looking at him as if pleading for him to "just keep your mouth shut."

He put on his professional face, turned back to look at Josh, and said, with a rather professional smile, "Hello, Josh, I'm Dr. Wilder, and I've been checking your progress as you've slept the hours away. You've made a miraculous recovery, but I don't think I'll be releasing you from the hospital today. You could possibly have a relapse after such a sudden awakening, so I'd like to keep you another 24 hours and take a few more tests. Are you having any pain in your eyes or head other than from the big goose egg you have back there? I'm sure it's pretty sore to the touch."

"No Sir, my eyes feel like I just woke up from a nice long nap. Except for my ribs hurting a little and the lump on my head throbbing when I touch it, I feel pretty good. I see I did a little damage to my arm, too, which means I won't be on the football field this season."

"It was a clean break, so it should heal pretty fast with no lasting difficulty, but I don't think I'd advise much football this coming season. Your ribs will give you the most pain for the next few weeks, though, since there's not much we can do to hurry the healing."

Liz had explained to Josh that his parents felt compelled to go home this morning, but Jon would be coming to see him. He certainly understood that because a farm just doesn't run by itself. "I wonder if I could talk to my brother at the Hayes Law Firm?" he asked, but then got a concerned look on his face. "I just realized that I don't know the number because I haven't called him there before, and I'm not even sure where I'm at," he chuckled.

Liz quickly spoke up, "I know the number, Josh, because I call Grandpa Noah quite often just to say hello. The answer to your remark about not being sure where you are is Colorado Springs. Dad felt this was the best hospital for you with Dr. Wilder on staff."

Dan was finally starting to put the family connections together. Noah Hayes, the eldest of the Ranch family, since the deaths of the patriarchs Nathaniel and Jeremiah, was her grandfather, as he was Christy's. He was recognizing the look alike features, too, except for the eyes, of Liz and Christy whom he now realized would be cousins. He'd also been told by Tim, his cousin who'd brought Josh to the hospital, that Jon Holcomb, his patient's brother, had been hired a few months ago at the Hayes Law Firm and that Christy was working there as a paralegal since graduating from college last year.

"I'll let you feed him some more ice chips, Liz, until his voice is a little stronger, and then you may handle the phone call. I'll be back later to check on Josh who is most likely about ready for some nourishment. How would you like for me to have a big plate of our delicious soft hospital food brought up to you?" he chuckled.

"That would be great, Dr. Wilder. My stomach does seem a little empty, but could it include some mashed potatoes, at least, if I have to tolerate that mushy stuff they call food?"

"I'll see what I can do, Josh, and I'll instruct them to go easy on you. That's not, of course, guaranteeing that you'll receive a steak dinner." He was smiling, as he left the room, realizing that he had taken quite a liking to this young man. Consequently, that evening, he'd spent longer than usual visiting with him on his late night rounds.

On Wednesday, when Dr. Wilder reached the door to Josh's room, he heard the most captivating voice coming from inside. When he glanced in, however, he only saw Liz sitting in a chair by the window, but then his eyes were quickly drawn to the nurse standing beside the bed. She was talking quietly to Josh as she took his vitals. She was rather tall, a really beautiful woman about 5'8" he would guess, with her long silky brunette hair falling to her shoulders.

As he listened from the hallway, she was telling Josh about her soldier husband being killed in Iraq last year, and that she'd probably have to sell the acreage they were buying and move into an apartment, which she was dreading. She'd also mentioned her dilemma about what to do with the two horses she owned. When he'd first seen her, Dan's heart had started beating like a young lion on its first hunt, but with his luck, could he possibly be able to help her with the acreage and the horses?

He then heard her say, "I shouldn't be telling you all this, Josh. My job now is to care for my patients, and I'd better be getting along. I'll see you on my next round."

Dr. Wilder had finally found his voice and walked in. With an inquisitive look on his face, he remarked, "I couldn't help overhearing some of your conversation with Josh, and I am truly interested in hearing more of your story." This beautiful nurse suddenly looked as if she might faint, and he instinctively took hold of her arm to steady her. She seemed quite startled with that move, however, and immediately pulled away. He then looked into her unusually bright blue eyes and quickly apologized. "I'm sorry if I frightened you. I'm just the surgeon who had to patch Josh up when he got a little careless horseback riding on the holiday." He smiled at Josh, and then turned back to her. "I'm Dr. Dan Wilder, coming to see if I can let my patient go home today. I don't believe we've met, so I'm assuming that this is your first day on this floor, Monica." He'd taken a quick glance at the name tag she wore on her uniform.

"Yes, Dr. Wilder, and I must apologize for taking so long with Josh. His vitals are all normal, and he certainly ate well this morning. I'd better get to my next patient now."

"I really would like to hear more of your story, Monica. Maybe we could meet later for a quick lunch. I could try to answer any questions you may have about the hospital or the routines by then. I'm again sorry I overheard some of your conversation with Josh, but I'd really like to learn more about our new employee, your loss, and the dilemma you have with the horses. I'll try to catch up with you later." He was rather surprised when she almost ran from the room. He hadn't had that reaction from any of the other nurses.

Monica could hardly get her breath by the time she'd reached the corridor outside the room, and she'd leaned against the wall as she tried to steady her nerves. All sorts of crazy thoughts were flying around in her head. *So, he's the Dr. Wilder, the unmarried surgeon all the nurses were talking about swooning over whenever he goes by the station or just looks at them? Now he has suggested we have lunch together because he wants to hear my story and see if he can answer any of the questions I might have? Why me?*

He isn't the most handsome man I've ever seen, although not bad. I'm not sure that I'd swoon if or when he looked at me, but maybe that's what he thought I was going to do when he took hold of my arm. He'd actually be quite good looking except for what I'd call a sad or lonely look, and also a stubborn looking square jaw. Maybe he's just all business and doesn't take much time for any fun or relaxation. He has to be over 6' tall and has that nice reddish tinge to his very thick and wavy ash blonde hair. With those expressive blue eyes, a beautiful tan and a very nice athletic build, how can he still be single? Almost any woman, other than me, would be thrilled to have him close to her, if only to perform an outpatient surgery procedure so she would be awake.

She quickly covered her mouth with her free hand as she started to giggle. *Oh,* she sighed, as she tightened her grip on the clipboard, *come on and get real, Monica, because he was most likely just being nice to a brand new employee. I'd better get moving now before he comes out of Josh's room and finds me still not to my next patient.*

Dr. Wilder had checked the chart, examined Josh's eyes, the lump on his head that is somewhat smaller than it had been yesterday, as well as his arm and ribs. "I think I can sign those release papers for you right after I've had lunch, Josh, but you'll need to see your own doctor as soon as you get home. Be sure to take it easy for a spell, and I wish you lots of luck in the future with those horses. I hope they don't give you any more trouble. I think you said it wasn't your first time on a horse. Is that right?"

"Yes, that's right, Dr. Wilder. I grew up on a farm and have been riding for years. This was just one of those freak accidents that happen when you take your mind and eyes off the trail." He looked at Liz with a big smile on his face and gave her a sexy wink.

"I'll remember that if I ever get the chance to ride one of those magnificent animals. I've enjoyed having you as a patient, Josh. Maybe we'll get to see each other again under a different set of circumstances." He started toward the door.

"I'd like that," Josh replied. He had taken in all the conversation between the doctor and Monica, and a grin was spreading across his face. If he wasn't still in a coma, then he was sure he had seen a case of infatuation in the doctor's eyes. Of course, that shocked look on Monica's face, when he'd taken hold of her arm, had really been something to see. *If I were a gambling man, I'd actually bet some money on the outcome of that relationship.* He felt that the doctor had looked pretty interested. He glanced over at Liz and could see that she was smiling and her brown eyes were twinkling. He wished she were in his arms but somewhere other than in a hospital room..

"What do you think, Pretty Lady? Is there a romance blossoming there?"

"Certainly sounded like a one-sided one to me. Dr. Wilder has always seemed like a pretty nice person, although a little too inquisitive at times, but Monica could certainly use a shoulder to lean on. Her story's really a sad one, and I hope she'll find happiness again."

Josh was going to question her remark about the doctor being too inquisitive, but he let it pass as he silently contemplated his future. *It's enough for me right now to realize I'm going home after this ordeal. Liz has been here with me, apparently, quite a bit of the time, and I'm still sort of thinking she might've kissed me, like a real fairy princess, to wake me up. I'd thought it had all been a nice dream, but maybe this cute little sweetheart likes me just a tad more than she thought she did at the Ranch. Right now she's being pretty secretive about all her actions and feelings, but I hope I'll learn the truth someday. I've certainly enjoyed getting to know her and hope we can at least have a great friendship.*

CHAPTER TWO

When he had finished his rounds, Dr. Wilder started toward his office to prepare for his 1 o'clock appointment, but then decided to stop by the nurses' station to see if he could catch Monica. Maybe he could persuade her to go to lunch even though her reaction to him this morning didn't give him lots of hope. He'd checked his schedule this morning and knew he only had three appointments this afternoon, so if the ER didn't have an emergency for him, his day would be fairly light. If not for lunch, then maybe she would have a cold drink with him in the cafeteria after her shift was over.

There were four nurses at the station and they were immediately smiling and wanting to help him. He had gotten used to the attention over the last three years since the two older surgeons had informed him, with his bachelor status, he would most likely be the topic of conversation at the nurses' station. He tried to smile at all of them but then asked, "Do you happen to know where Monica is?"

Knowing it was her first day, their first reaction was concern that she had possibly done something wrong and was in trouble. "Oh, Dr. Wilder, it's her first day on the floor. Maybe one of us should have been with her this morning," the head nurse, Trudy, remarked.

"No, she was doing fine when I met her earlier this morning. I just wanted to talk to her for a few minutes about another matter. I'll catch up with her later." He turned to walk to the elevators and heard the sighs. He just shook his head. *All in a day's work, I guess, but I wonder if I can be lucky enough to get that same reaction from Monica one day soon.*

About twenty minutes later, Monica approached the station so excited and smiling. "I have had the most wonderful morning. I know I'm going to love this job," she exclaimed but then noticed that the nurses had all turned and were staring at her. "What is it? Did I do something wrong?" she asked as she sat down to work on her reports.

"We're not sure," Ann said as she went to stand beside her. "Did you happen to meet Dr. Wilder this morning? He was looking for you and said he'd catch up with you later."

Now visibly upset, Monica started telling them what

had happened in Josh's room earlier this morning and she didn't really know what to make of it. "Josh had asked about my nursing career after I'd told him it was my first day. He'd jokingly hoped I wouldn't be more nervous because Liz, the cute young girl sitting with him, was Dr. Becker's daughter. I was telling him about the acreage that I would probably have to sell and find someplace for the horses when Dr. Wilder came in and said he would like to hear more of my story. I was so stunned that he must've thought I was going to faint because he took hold of my arm to help steady me. What am I going to do? I can't talk to him about my problems. Please, will you all help me?"

"Wow! I wish I had a problem that he wanted to hear more about," Trudy groaned but then laughed. "You have accomplished, on your first day, what the rest of us have been trying to do for three years. You know he's a bachelor, Monica, so if you find him attractive, don't run the other way. I've heard, via the grapevine, that he fell for a young girl about ten years ago, but then he left for his long, hard medical training and hasn't dated much at all."

Ann spoke up. "Oh, Monica, we'll all envy you, but actually, most of us already have a husband or a boyfriend or two, so we won't hate you. We just love to have fun making a fuss over him because he's the only unmarried doctor we have in surgery. Of course, being good looking and a handsome hunk certainly helps, don't you think? You do consider him good looking, don't you?"

"I really hadn't given it much thought. I've only seen him for a couple of minutes in Josh's room this morning and he didn't make me swoon, if that's what you're asking. I've got to have some time to think about this lunch invitation, though. Could I ask a favor of all of you? If he comes back asking for me, would you tell him I had an errand to run on my lunch hour and won't be back until after one? I just don't think I can face him again today."

"What if he comes back after one?" Ann asked jokingly. "You can't very easily hide from a doctor unless you're exceptionally good at hide and seek." And then with a big grin, she'd continued, "And exactly where do you think you're going to eat your lunch---in the restroom?"

"When am I supposed to go to lunch, anyway? We can't shut everything down, I realize that, so do we go two at a time, one at a time, or what is the routine?"

Trudy had just answered a room call and Ann had been summoned to talk to a family member of a patient, so Nancy walked over to her and answered her question. "Most of us bring our lunch, Monica, and eat in the nurses' lounge. Sometimes we go to the cafeteria, or on a nice day, we might slip out to the small café down the street or go out in the courtyard of the hospital. We can usually go two at a time, but it depends on what's happening here."

Ann had just returned from consoling the family member and quickly whispered to Monica, "Don't look now, but that unmarried doctor, who wants to see you, just got off the elevator. If you're sure you don't want to see him, you'd better scoot. Just go down the B corridor and slip into the restroom."

With Dr. Wilder's long legs, Monica barely got out of sight before he'd reached the station. "I see she's still not around unless you're all hiding her someplace. As I told all you ladies, she's not in trouble. I just want to talk to her about something I overheard her talking to Josh Holcomb about this morning. By the way, I need to sign the discharge papers for that young man. He really made a remarkable recovery, didn't he?" Unable to stop his grin and a little chuckle, he took the papers Ann handed him and got the release completed. "He and Liz may stay in his room part of the afternoon because Josh has to wait for his brother to come pick him up."

"Will they be bringing a lunch tray for him, then?" Nancy asked.

"Yes, I ordered one for him and one for Liz. I hope they don't reprimand me for that," he chuckled. "O.K., Ladies, since you aren't going to help me with Monica, I'll have to find some other way to solve her dilemma. I don't give up very easily when I'm on a mission." He turned and walked toward the elevators.

Ann ran down the hall to the restroom to retrieve Monica. "It's not going to be easy for you to escape him. He says he's on a mission to solve your dilemma and he doesn't give up easily. Oh, Monica, maybe he just wants to help you save the farm, or maybe he knows someplace you could take the horses. You really need to talk to him."

"I suppose, Ann, but right after losing Terry, I couldn't look at another man without crying. I'd try to go out to eat with my friends, walk down the street to shop, or even go to church on Sundays, and I'd always end up crying. I'm not sure I'm ready to sit down and talk to any man about my problems, let alone a stranger."

As they made their way back to the station, Ann remarked, "You seemed to be able to do that very thing with Josh this morning. He's a very handsome guy, too, but I think Liz has him wrapped around her little finger, although it may be the other way around. She is such a precious little girl, only sixteen, but so mature for her age. She comes to the hospital a lot with her dad and just loves talking to some of the older patients who don't have very many visitors. I think I saw on Josh's chart that he is 21, so she has her work cut out for her, if she's really serious about him."

"He is certainly a nice guy. He so easily put me at ease

when I entered his room and was so nervous. Liz just sat and listened, but she didn't interfere with my checking his vitals or anything. Being a doctor's daughter, she could've been a know-it-all."

"Not Liz Becker, no way. She is the sweetest, most considerate and most friendly young girl I have ever met. From what I hear, the whole family is like that, from the grand-father right on down. In fact, they say the great, great grandfather was always doing things for the town he'd helped settle. They belong to the Haven of Rest Ranch family, of Hayes, by the way, if you didn't know."

"No, I didn't know that, but I have heard about the ranch and all the good they have done for their town and the area."

Trudy was waiting, when they got back. "Well, it appears you dodged the bullet this time, Monica, but I think you'd better get ready for a conversation with Dr. Wilder. I saw him enter the elevator and he had that determined look in his eyes, and I don't think he's going to give up."

Angela, who had said nothing during the whole episode, pushed her chair back from the desk, where she'd been working on her reports. She said, quite disgustedly, "Well, I'm going to lunch, not that any of you will miss me. It appears that Monica has been able to grab the limelight on her very first day, but I just hope she can keep her mind on her work and her patients and not cause a catastrophe." She marched off with her lunch sack swinging rather roughly in her hand.

"What was that all about?" Nancy asked quite innocently as she continued to watch Angela stomp off toward the lounge. This was the first time she had worked with Angela who had only been on this floor for the past two or three weeks.

"I'm afraid that's just Angela wanting to be the center of attraction," Trudy remarked. She and Ann were trying not to laugh as they remembered an incident shortly after Angela had joined them. They were quickly brought back to attention when the buzzer sounded.

"Nurse's Station, this is Ann. How may we help you?"

"I need help, please."

"I'll be right there," and Ann was down the hall on a run.

Another buzzer. Trudy answered and heard a young man's voice asking if Dr. Wilder had signed his discharge papers. "I want to call my brother and see when he can come to get me if I'm going to be allowed to leave."

"The papers are signed, Josh, and I'll have Monica bring them to you right away."

"Thanks, you ladies must have taken very good care of me while I was taking a nice long nap. I feel great now so I'll have to think of something extra special to do for you." With a little chuckle, he whispered, "Maybe I could give you all one of my special kisses."

"We'd probably all enjoy that," Trudy laughed, "but we do have to be very careful about spreading germs around the hospital. It's been a pleasure having you with us, Josh. Monica will be right there, and you be very careful around those horses, you hear?"

Monica took the discharge papers and headed for Josh's room. She was glad she'd see him again before he left. He'd really helped get her first day off to a wonderful start.

She'd just delivered the papers and was wishing him a speedy recovery when she sensed that someone else was coming into the room. She looked up and gasped. *Is someone playing a mean trick on me or what?* She turned and frowned at Josh, when she'd heard him chuckle. Of course, his cute grin caused an unwanted smile, but she also knew her following remark had sounded a bit forced. "I'd better let your doctor see you now. Goodbye, Josh."

She then glanced at Dr. Wilder. She could tell, with the surprised look on his face, that he hadn't deliberately planned this surprise meeting, but had Josh? She looked again at the smiling face lying so innocently on the bed. As she started to move away, Josh grabbed her hand, brought it to his lips and kissed it. "It was great meeting you, Monica, and I really hope everything works out for you." Pulling her toward him, he softly whispered so only she could hear, "Don't be too afraid of the doctor. Those guys have different ways of doing their thing, but they are usually rather tender hearted when it comes to people they like." He had her close enough now that he kissed her cheek before he released her hand.

"Thanks, Josh, I'll take that under advisement," she whispered with a scowl. She then turned to Liz and said, "I'm so glad I got the chance to meet you, Liz. Maybe we'll see each other here at the hospital now and then."

She started toward the door, but her path was being blocked by Dr. Wilder who had his arm outstretched and his hand against the wall. "I-I'm so sar-sorry," she stammered, "but I-I have to ge-get back to the nur-nurses' sta-station." She'd heard Josh chuckle again and so she turned to look at him with a deep, disturbing frown, but that smile softened her face into a big uncontrollable grin. "I'll not forget you, Josh," she uttered in an almost silent whisper as she turned back to face this arm that was still preventing her from leaving.

"I just thought I'd drop in to tell Josh goodbye before I went to my office for a couple of appointments this afternoon, but it is an added pleasure to see you again. I was beginning to think you were avoiding me. I guess I shouldn't have listened to your conversation with Josh this morning, but I didn't do it intentionally. I heard your voice when I got to the door, and decided I shouldn't intrude. I'm so sorry about the loss of your husband and your current indefinite plans about the farm and the horses. My one dream, when I was growing up, was to own a horse, or just ride one, but my father wouldn't let me do either. So, would there be any chance that you'd just talk to me? I'd really like to help if I can."

"You are persistent, if not very persuasive, Dr. Wilder, but would you give me some time to consider it? My life has been pretty hectic this last year and I've had a rather hard time talking to anyone, let alone a stranger. We'll probably be seeing each other, since we're both going to be at this hospital almost every day, so maybe you could give me a few days?"

"Oh, certainly, Monica. I'm sorry if I seemed a little pushy. I didn't mean to come across that way. I'm just anxious to get to know you and welcome you to the hospital. We'll see each other soon." He slowly dropped his arm from the wall to allow her to leave, but he couldn't keep from turning and watching her walk away. He smiled as he thought about the nurses doing the same thing to him.

He turned now to his patient. "I assume you've made arrangements to be picked up, Josh. I just wanted to wish you well. I enjoyed having you as a patient and our private talk, also meeting your family and your little friend here. It appears you have also made a hit with your nurse today. You wouldn't want to share your secret with me, would you? I don't seem to be having any luck getting acquainted with her."

"I'm afraid my success with Monica is that there were no strings attached because I'm a little younger, I had Liz here with me, and I'm leaving the hospital soon. I got her talking about her nursing career first, and that led to her telling me about losing her husband in Iraq last year. I've heard that you have all the nurses swooning, so she has probably heard more than enough about you. How *is* your reputation, Doctor? Are you just a playboy who's found another pretty lady to chase, if I can be so bold to ask? I hope not, because she really needs time to get adjusted to her new job, get to know you as just a friend, and receive a lot of understanding from all those around her."

"No, Josh, I'm no playboy, and I felt like I was hit with a ton of bricks when I saw her in your room this morning. I'd love to get to know her and try to help her save her home and the horses, if I can."

"All I can say is, relax and don't rush her. She's had a huge loss and probably still needs time to get used to being alone. If you could be someone she could rely on, though, it'd most likely go a long way toward a relationship, if that's what you really want."

"Thanks, Josh, I'll remember all your thoughts. You sound much older and wiser than your chart indicates. God's speed with your healing and just remember those ribs will also take time and maybe a lot of understanding, too," he laughed.

After the doctor had left the room, Josh motioned for Liz to come to his right side of the bed. "I think there's a future for those two, don't you?" He put his good arm around her waist and pulled her to him.

"Maybe so. It appears that they both could use some tender, loving care, and they certainly know how to give it to their patients. Hopefully they can confide in each other and maybe find the love together that they've lost in previous relationships."

"Wow, you should write for the lovelorn column," he chuckled.

CHAPTER THREE

Monica was so confused with all that was happening on her first day of work, she was afraid she'd made some mistake that would come crashing down on her head. Now, she had just finished the last vitals check and her shift would soon be over. She could go home and try to figure out just what was going on. She'd seen Josh's brother, Jon, come with a huge bouquet of flowers for the nurses' station, and they had left with Liz about a half-hour ago. Jon was just as handsome as Josh, and there was no denying that they were brothers. *Two very lucky girls are going to catch them for their husbands one of these days,* she mused.

All of her other patients were doing fine and probably would be leaving for home in a day or two, so she punched out and headed toward her comfortable little bungalow northeast of the city. She and Terry had worked so hard to fix it up after they'd been able to buy it dirt cheap from the owner who had gotten himself too deeply in debt. He'd originally owned 500 acres, but had sold them off, a few at a time, to pay his gambling debts. There were only the 10 acres left, along with the neglected little house, when he finally went for treatment and then decided to move nearer his family.

After two years of satisfying work, Terry, who'd been in the Reserves, was called to go to Iraq. He'd been so confident he'd be back and they could resume their life together, but then he'd been killed. His parents had really been so supportive, but recently they had urged her to go on with her life. They all knew that was what Terry would have wanted. So, now she is a nurse, the career she had wanted even as a teenager, although she would never regret the years she had spent as his wife.

When Dan had finished with his appointments for the day, he quickly slipped into the Mercedes-Benz convertible, that he had leased, and just started driving. He wanted so badly to go find the place that this Monica called home, but he had promised to give her time and he intended to do just that. It wasn't going to be easy, he'd realized, as the hours had passed.

She'd caused all kinds of vibes to go through my body, especially when I'd gotten the chance to look into those eyes. They change from a bright blue to a deep blue and at times,

I thought, they looked almost black. They were incredible and so was she. Her shyness, or a sadness, had come through loud and clear, but I hadn't really grasped it until I'd seen her the second time in Josh's room. I'm ashamed of myself for not understanding her needs and just pushing forward with my own agenda. I'll have to think of some way to make it up to her.

He had the top down on his car, and the wind was blowing through his thick wavy hair on this hot but beautiful July day. He was meandering through the city streets without a purpose, he'd thought, until, all at once, he found himself on the outskirts--the northeast out- skirts. He'd checked out her address in the phone book, and if he was anywhere near right, he should be fairly close to that area.

So what are you doing out here? that little voice was whispering to him, but he just couldn't stop himself--he had to know where she lived. *I won't bother her,* he vows as he turns onto an old blacktop road and assumes the one he's looking for isn't far from here.

He'd gone by quite a development of homes and a good sized mall back a ways, and he began to wonder if he had made a wrong turn. He finally saw the name of her street, or more like an unpaved country road, he quickly realized, as he turned onto it. He wished he had the top up now because this was one dusty road, and he's going to spend some good money getting the car cleaned after this little jaunt of curiosity.

He had only driven about a mile when all of a sudden the road stopped. He could do nothing but turn into a driveway where he looked into the shocked eyes of the one and only Monica Reynolds. She was standing, apparently, where she had been tending a garden of beautiful flowers. He'd never felt more like a fool than he did at that moment. *Okay, Dandy Dan, what are you going to do now?* He knew he had to face her, so he slowly opened the car door while he was thinking, and still thinking, *what **am** I going to say?*

"Well, fancy meeting you here," he blurts out, being at a loss for words. "It was such a beautiful day that I decided to take a little ride and let the wind blow through my hair, and look where I ended up. Oh, Monica, I feel like an absolute fool. I just wanted to see where you lived and, maybe get a peek at the horses. I never dreamed that it would be a dead-end road and I would be caught red faced with nowhere to hide. Can you ever forgive me?"

By this time, she couldn't keep from laughing at his feeble attempt to explain why he was in her driveway. "Well, Dr. Wilder, I do believe that you gave your car a good dust bath this afternoon, and you'll probably need a good long shower when you get home. As long as you're here, come in and I'll fix you a cool drink. Would you prefer lemonade or iced tea?"

"I really shouldn't impose, but my throat feels like I've inhaled about a fourth of the dust on your road. So, if you really don't mind, I'll take you up on that drink. Which would be easier for you to fix? You should just give me plain water."

"I actually have both in the fridge, Dr. Wilder. I'm almost always thirsty, since I live on this dusty road, so I keep a good supply of liquids cold and ready."

She was terribly nervous when they'd reached the door to her sun porch, and she did hesitate before she motioned for him to come on in. *He is a doctor, after all, and he's not a complete stranger,* she'd tried to rectify her decision.

He'd noticed that it was a very cozy room with windows on three sides to view the manicured back yard, which looked as if a professional had done the landscaping. He stood admiring all the plantings until he realized she was talking to him.

"Have you decided which you would like, Dr. Wilder?" she asked again but she was following his eyes surveying the yard. "Terry and I spent almost three weeks drawing the plans before we started planting all the shrubs, trees and flowers. He'd wanted to use the south acreage for his greenhouses and all the other things you need for landscaping, leaving the area to the north for riding and a large yard. The large yard, unfortunately, was all we got a good start on after spending so much time on the house to make it livable."

"You did a great job, Monica, and iced tea would be fine if it's not too much trouble. I am so embarrassed to have driven out here. I feel like I should crawl in a hole."

"Forget it, Dr. Wilder, you are here now, you need a cool drink, and I want to be a gracious hostess. I'll get you some iced tea."

She was back shortly with two glasses of tea and a plate of cookies on a tray. "I forgot to ask if you wanted sugar for your tea, Dr. Wilder. I drink everything plain so I forget to ask most of the time. Would you like some sugar or lemon for yours?"

"No, this is fine, Monica, but there is a favor I'd like to ask of you. Although I'm just a little hesitant, I'm going to ask it anyway. Would you possibly consider calling me Dan? It doesn't seem quite right to be called Dr. Wilder by someone I want as a friend."

There was that shocked look again. "Can I do that at the hospital? I assumed that it was pretty formal between doctors and nurses there."

"As we get to know each other more personally around the hospital, the doctors and a few of the nurses call each other by their first names. If you would feel better calling me Dr. Wilder at the hospital, that's fine, but what about right here, now?"

"Oh, I see. You think it's a little formal to call you Dr. Wilder when you're sitting in my home and we're drinking iced tea together?" She giggled and he wanted to just give her a great big hug. He was more than a little puzzled at this sudden reaction to a woman, after his years of being alone, but he also loved the feelings he was experiencing.

Conversation flowed easily between them for almost an hour, but she'd stammered a little as she'd tried to remember to call him Dan. "I'm afraid it's going to take me awhile to get used to calling you Dan, but I was going to ask if you'd like to go and see my two horses. I haven't been to the barn yet this afternoon and they'll be expecting me." She couldn't stop her grin as she watched his reaction to her offer.

Dan had jumped up from the couch like a little child because he was so excited, and all kinds of thoughts were racing through his head. In all the times he'd gone to the Ranch to watch the activities, he'd never dared go see if he could touch one of the horses. He'd been too afraid his dad would recognize the smell of the horse on him and then he would've been banned from going to the Ranch ever again. Now, here he is, 33 years old, getting his first chance at being close to his favorite animal.

Feeling foolish, but not wanting to do anything

wrong, he asked, "Monica, is there anything special I should or shouldn't do when I get close to the horses?"

"Is this the first time you've ever been close enough to touch a horse? I would have thought, when you told me about going to the Ranch, that you would've been given the grand tour." As she watched him shake his head, she continued, "Well, this isn't the Haven of Rest Ranch, Dan, but you're going to be able to be near Rascal and Tumbleweed. Maybe we'll go saddle them up for a short ride and then you can help feed them, brush them down, and above all, talk to them. Give me your hand, and I'll give you your first lesson on caring for a horse."

He was surprised how natural it seemed to be holding hands with this most beautiful woman whom he'd just met this morning. Everything continued to be perfect for him---his first touch of a horse, Monica showing him how to put the saddle on, the ride, the cooling down and the feeding. He'd felt as though he were in heaven, and when they'd finished the chores and went out of the barn, he then realized that the sun was setting.

"Wow, I'd better get headed back to the city. I never dreamed I had imposed on your hospitality this long, but I've certainly enjoyed my first time with you and with the horses."

"You're probably about starved after all that exercise, so why don't you let me fix us some supper? I'll let you help me wash and dry the dishes since there isn't a dishwasher."

"No dishwasher? How do you live without a dishwasher?" With a hearty laugh, he grabbed her hand and they almost ran to the house to share their first meal together.

Without hesitation, Monica started fixing a very easy chicken skillet meal. "I used to make this a lot," she remarked, "when Terry and I had spent too much time working on the house or yard and needed a quick dinner." The chicken had been browned slightly and then she had poured a simple sauce over it, which was made with cream of chicken soup and just a little cooking Sherry, and then she'd added some green beans and mushrooms. She put the water on to boil for minute rice, and while the chicken and rice were cooking, she'd tossed a salad. The sauce she'd put over the chicken to simmer would be used as a topping for the rice.

Dan had wanted to help so she had him set the table and get the drinks ready. They were seated and ready to eat when she reached for his hand but then quickly drew it back. Dan, however, had noticed and wasn't going to let it go.

"What did you mean to do, Monica, when you reached for my hand? I've lived alone for so long, please let me in on some of the traditions that are important to you."

"Terry and I always held hands when we prayed before our meals. It is a tradition of his family, and he'd wanted to continue it with just the two of us so we wouldn't be out of the habit when children came along. I'm sorry, but it just seemed right when there was someone sitting at the table with me."

"Don't be sorry for wanting to continue a tradition that is family oriented. If you want to pray, I'll be more than happy to hold your hand and even add a few words of my own."

She reached over again and he took her hand, they bowed their heads and she said a short prayer. Then Dan, squeezing her hand, prayed, "I want to thank you, Dear Lord, for one of the most exciting days of my life, even after making a fool of myself by driving out here to see where Monica lives. I am thankful for her forgiveness and for the chance you've given me to meet her and share this meal with her. Watch over us, Dear Jesus, as we care for the sick, and may our lives enhance one another. Amen."

Their conversation went smoothly, and she was delighted that he offered, without her even asking, stories about his growing up in Hayes, and then on to the medical training. He put his fork down and looked at her with a sadness that she could not read, but then he said,

"I wasn't raised in a Christian home, Monica, and I

feel that I missed a lot of the closeness a family should have. My father and mother, when together, were very distant toward me, and since I was an only child, I was mostly kept out of their presence by a nanny. We did attend church occasionally, like at Christmas and Easter, but I didn't go to Sunday School where I could've learned about the life and love of Jesus.

Fortunately, I had a roommate in Med School who invited me to go to church with him. Actually, it started with a Singles Group that met once a month, and then, one Sunday, I asked if I could go to worship with him. I became a Christian not long after that, but when you're by yourself, you let a lot of that stuff slip."

"Thanks, Da-Dan, for sharing that with me. My growing up years were difficult, too.

I never realized how much my mother put up with trying to keep the home together for my brother and me, taking us to Sunday School and Worship, going to all of our activities by herself, and never was there a bad word about Dad. Instead, she always had an excuse why he wasn't there.

But then, out of the blue, when I was a junior in high school and my brother was in his first year of college, Dad packed his things in the back of his pickup and took off. We haven't heard from him since. He did leave a trust that specifically paid for our two college tuitions, but nothing except the house, with a mortgage, and what was in the checkbook did he leave for Mom.

After I graduated, she sold the house and we moved into a small apartment. She was fortunate to have a friend who had helped her find a job at a Travel Agency, and she is still there. She loves the job, and the apartment is plenty large for her without me crowding her space," she giggled but then continued. "I went to college for two years and then entered the Nurses Training School. It was about six months before my graduation when I met Terry at a wedding reception of mutual friends, and we were married a year later."

Smiling, she looked at him and remarked, "I think we've just shared a big piece of our life stories tonight, Dan, and I'm so glad we've met. As you know, this last year has been a very hard one for me, and I don't have a lot of friends to spend time with. Oh, I do have two very close friends, but they're so busy with their own jobs, plus their homes and husbands, it's hard to get together. We've tried to meet for lunch occasionally, and I sit with them at church, but it just isn't the same. Do you know what I mean?"

"I understand, Monica, although I didn't have to face the death of a loved one. My loneliness has been pretty much self-imposed because I thought I wanted it that way. I have a close cousin, who is an EMT in Hayes, and we get together now and then to catch up on family and friends we grew up with. I haven't any close friends in the hospital, although the doctors are all great. It's just that, like you, they have their wives and families and so a very different kind of life away from the hospital."

They had finished eating some time ago, but finally Monica got up to start clearing the table. Dan jumped up and had to grab his chair as he almost tipped it over in his hurry to help. She just looked at him and grinned. "You probably should be getting back home as it's really getting late for a doctor to be out roaming around in a convertible, don't you think? I can do the dishes and clean up the kitchen."

"No way, Madame," he said as he made a sweeping bow from the waist and grabbed a towel from the rack. "It is my duty to help my exceptional hostess clean up her lovely kitchen in which she so graciously cooked and served a most delicious meal."

Monica couldn't believe this was a distinguished doctor who had her laughing with his performing arts, so to speak, and he was mesmerized by her dancing eyes. Working together, they made short work of the kitchen and had it sparkling once again. He was so reluctant to leave, but he didn't want to overstay his welcome either, so he thanked her again for everything, and then, without thinking, he started to pull her into his arms.

Only his pager going off kept him from making a fool of himself again. "May I use your phone to call the hospital?" he asked. He quickly learned there was an accident victim who desperately needed his expertise. He explained that he was about 30 minutes away but would be there as fast as he could. He was sorry he didn't have a siren to turn on so traffic would let him have the right-of-way. He was dashing toward the door as he said, "Goodbye" to Monica and was on his way.

He had just reached the highway when he spotted a patrol car sitting in the nearby cafe parking lot. *Would it be permitted?* he was wondering, but his car seemed to head there on its own. In seconds, he was being led through the traffic at a pretty good clip, and he was in the Operating Room in less than 15 minutes. God must have known time was critical and had the patrol car waiting there because a few minutes delay would have meant disaster that night in the OR. It was long after midnight when he'd left the hospital.

He sank into his recliner, but he could only think about calling Monica. *Would she still be up and maybe wondering about the victim?* he pondered. He reached for the phone but then realized he didn't even have her number. He dug the telephone directory out of the lamp table drawer and found the listing. He dialed and was surprised when it was answered after the first ring.

"Hello, is that you, Dan?"

"Yes, Monica, it is. How did you know I would call and that this was me?"

"Well, I don't get too many phone calls after midnight," she giggled, "but I've been praying so hard that you'd get there in time and that you'd let me know how everything went. I wouldn't have been able to sleep, otherwise. I'd called about 45 minutes ago and was just getting ready to call again to see if you were home yet. I would've kept calling until I had reached you, even if it'd meant waking you up. How did it go? Please tell me everything."

He couldn't believe that someone would be so interested in what he was doing, and it made him all the more intrigued. He told her about the patrol car, the race through the city streets, the nip and tuck of the difficult surgery, and that another accident victim had been saved by an act of God.

"We are so blessed to have His guiding hand to help us, aren't we?"

"Yes, Monica, and your prayers were most likely helping, too."

CHAPTER FOUR

The days following the great time he'd had with Monica were filled with far more emergency surgeries than Dan had seen for quite a while. He had thought the 4th of July weekend would've been pretty bad with accident victims, but it had been rather slow. Even though he'd scheduled the holiday off, he'd somehow known he'd be called in before the day was over. And sure enough, he'd been called in because of Josh Holcomb being thrown from the horse he'd been riding.

I'm really glad I didn't miss that young man and his cute fairy princess, he mused, *but these last three days have actually been a rough combination of car accidents, an open heart surgery, two appendectomies, a gall bladder surgery, and a few broken limbs. I had hoped I might see Monica in the halls, at least, but she has apparently been as busy, or busier, than I have.*

It was now late Sunday afternoon, he had just finished his rounds, and he was looking forward to dropping into his old favorite recliner. He was almost to the door of the doctor's parking lot when he heard his name being called. He mumbled, "I can't do one more thing today," but he turned around and saw one of the nurses from Monica's floor hurrying toward him. *Her name is Angela, I think, but what would she want with me? Oh, No, something hasn't happened to Monica, has it?"*

She reached his side with a huge smile on her face. She seemed a little flushed, but he just wanted to hear what she had to say so he could go home. Her smile had wiped away the fear of Monica being in trouble. "What is it?" he asked a little impatiently.

She hesitated a moment and he thought her cheeks had reddened a little more, but then she blurted out rapidly, "Aah--I--was wondering if I could talk to you about something I think is quite important for you to hear."

"And just what would that be? Your name is Angela, isn't it?"

"Yes, I'm Angela." *I can't believe he doesn't know my name, but he will soon enough.* "I think you should know that this Monica Reynolds, the nurse who just started working on Wednesday and acted so innocent, already has plans for snagging a new man for herself. She came to work Thursday morning with the biggest smile on her face. As she proceeded to talk to Ann and Trudy, who have become her best buddies, it was pretty clear to me that she had an agenda all mapped out. So much for playing the poor, shy and grieving widow. It doesn't take a genius to figure out for whom that trap is set. I could see you just wanted to talk to her about some hospital matter, but she apparently took it as a romantic interest. I thought I'd warn you to watch out for this Monica Reynolds because I'm sure she's after you.

I'm asking for a transfer to ICU next week," she continued, "so I'll be working closer to you, Dr. Wilder. If you have time to have a cold drink with me, I'd love to tell you about my training and how I'll be an asset to the unit." She waited for him to accept her invitation with all the confidence of a true egotist.

"I'm glad to hear your version of what went on at the nurses' station, Angela, and you just leave it to me. I'll take care of Monica the best I know how. As for your transfer, I wish you luck in your new endeavor. I'm sure you'll do fine. However, these last few days have been hectic and I'm heading home to crash. I'm sorry I can't hear the wonderful enlightening story of all your talents. Goodnight, Angela."

Angela couldn't keep from smiling as she headed to the cafeteria alone for that cold drink. *I'm sure he bought it all about that smug and conniving Monica Reynolds, so now she won't stand a chance. She might fool Trudy and Ann, but Dr. Dan Wilder will be under my spell once I'm in ICU and working close to him. It won't be long until he's anxious to spend a lot of time with me once I start my come-on tactics. After all, I've been a nurse for over four years, and I'll have a lot more to talk to the doctor about than a new inexperienced nurse like her. I would guess I'm at least two or three years younger, much prettier, and most likely a lot more talented in the ways to satisfy a man. I think she's only had her husband to teach her, which, in my eyes, is a very dull way to learn about sex.* Angela's vivid imagination was definitely causing romantic emotions as she sipped her drink.

Dan was so tired, but when he got to his car, he folded his arms over the top of the steering wheel and had a good laugh. *I just hope that one thing she said was true,* he gasped as he got his breath between laughs, *and that is that Monica came to work Thursday with a smile on her face.* He had been concerned that she would consider him an absolute idiot and want nothing to do with him. What would he have done then when he had felt so captivated by her? If she was happy, he hoped it meant that she'd enjoyed being with him Wednesday night and would consider spending a lot more time with him.

Oh, Monica, I wish I had the strength to drive out to your place and see you tonight, but I'm afraid I would be very poor company this time. Of course, if I could fall asleep with my head in your lap, it would be worth the drive, but on the other hand, as tired as I am, I might have an accident trying to get there. I'll just play it safe, go home and dream.

He wasn't in his chair over two minutes when he was sound asleep. His dreams were wonderful and he was finally holding Monica and getting the kiss he'd missed on Wednesday night. He suddenly was awakened sputtering and spitting, however, and realized that a dog was licking his face. "What the devil is going on and where did you come from?" he yelled as he jumped up from his chair and pushed the dog away. He then heard the familiar laugh that belonged to his cousin. He was about ready to tackle the guy, but it was always good to see Tim. "What are you doing in town, and where did you pick up that mongrel?"

"Hey, he's no mongrel. He may be an orphan, but he's clean, groomed, and has a new home--mine! Actually, Gene and I found him the other day wandering around the back yards in the neighborhood, about starved, and pretty straggly. There were no tags, but he is well trained. He sits, heels, and goes to the door when he needs to go out. What more can you ask from a roommate?"

"What happens while you're at work? Please don't tell me you take him on all your Rescue calls."

"Sometimes, like tonight, but the back yard is fenced in, you know, and there's the one big tree plus some pretty tall bushes to give him shade. The landlord said I could let him stay in there as long as I built a house so he could get in out of the bad weather. Gene and I have spent the last few days building a doghouse at the station because it's been pretty slow. By the way, how's that Holcomb boy? Have you let him go home yet?"

"Yep, he went home Wednesday afternoon. That was one patient, and his cute little visitor, that I really enjoyed. There has to be quite an age difference there, but if they don't get together one day, I'll really be surprised."

"Did you get to see anymore of Christy?"

"Who's Christy?" he chuckled. "I'll have to tell you about my experience Wednesday afternoon and evening. Actually it started in the morning on my rounds. I was thrilled, then I made a fool of myself, and then I was forgiven, taken on a horseback ride, served a great homemade dinner, and enjoyed learning about the most beautiful woman I've ever laid eyes on." He elaborated on the evening until Tim had been told the whole blissful experience Dan had had with Monica and seemed to be reliving it all again.

"Wow, when you fall, you really fall, don't you? Well, I wish you all the luck in the world, Dan. You really deserve it. I've even been thinking about giving Kate a ring. We've been dating for four years now, so I guess I should start getting a little more serious."

"That'd be great news, Tim. I've always liked Kate, and I think she'd be good for you. A loving wife to go home to at night is starting to sound very appealing, and maybe I'll get to follow you to the altar if I can keep my head on straight."

"From what you've told me, this Monica sounds great and I'm looking forward to meeting her. But I've got to go now. We delivered Mrs. Wichard to the hospital tonight for surgery in the morning. Is she your patient?"

"Yeah, and I'd better get some more sleep. I would hate to make a mistake on that sweet elderly lady. Is she still living alone in that big old house?"

"No, she's living in that new retirement home that Dr. Noland had built. It was just opened about six or eight months ago and Mrs. Wichard was one of the first to move in. It's really one beautiful place, including the assisted living and nursing wings when the residents need the extra care. He must've had a great architect drawing the plans for him. It appears to have everything a person would need for enjoying life to the fullest as you grow older, and then taken good care of to your very last breath."

"Leave it to Dr. Noland to know exactly what the little town needs. Have a safe trip home, Tim. Hey, what did you name the mongrel?"

"Lucky. Goodnight, Dan."

"Goodnight, Tim."

Lucky, that's exactly what I am. Very, very lucky.

CHAPTER FIVE

After Tim left, Dan realized that he hadn't eaten anything when he'd gotten home and his stomach was starting to tell him. He fixed himself a sandwich, chips, and an apple and watched the news while he ate. He glanced at the clock and saw that it was a little past nine o'clock. *Would Monica still be up? I'd love to hear her voice and find out how her last few days have gone. Better than mine, I hope.* Hesitating for just a moment, he picked up the phone and dialed.

After seven rings, he was about to hang up when he heard the receiver being lifted off the cradle. "Hey, Reynolds' residence," she said sounding a little out of breath.

"Hey, yourself. What took you so long to answer, or am I being a little too nosey? I am sorry to be calling so late, but I came home and fell asleep. I'd probably still be asleep, but my cousin came in with a new dog he'd found the other day. He actually let it wake me up by licking my face. I'd been dreaming that I was holding you and getting the kiss that I was robbed of the other night, but that dog's licking kiss was no substitute for the one I'm hoping to get from you one day soon."

She couldn't hold back the giggle as she could just imagine being awakened by a dog licking her face. "I was just coming in from the barn when I heard the phone ringing, and I was afraid I might miss it. My friend, Charlotte, was supposed to get in touch with me, so I thought she might be calling. I'm glad it was you, though, because I've been wondering how the rest of your week went. I'd noticed your name on a lot of the charts so I knew you were having a full load, but I was surprised we hadn't at least seen each other in the halls or at the station."

"Aha, checking on me, huh? That's a felony, you know, and punishable by multiple kisses instead of just one." She could hear his chuckle before he continued, "So, you were out in the barn a little late tonight. Was there anything wrong?"

"No, nothing wrong. I just spent a little more time cleaning stalls while talking to my two best friends, Rascal and Tumbleweed. I had sort of neglected them because it has been pretty hectic on 4th floor, too. I'd been coming home and collapsing and then spending very little time at the barn. One of the nurses has been complaining of not feeling well, and she's been asking me to help check some of her patients. Not that I minded, but it did keep me a little extra busy on my shift."

"I understand that the one named Angela has or is going to request a transfer to ICU. I suppose that will make you short a nurse and increase the burden of the others. I sure hope they can replace her quickly."

"She hasn't said anything at the station that I know of, but she hasn't been too overly friendly or talkative around me. I tried, a few times, to find out what I'd done wrong, but she just shrugged her shoulders and walked away. Then, yesterday and today, she came to me and asked the favor of checking her patients."

"Don't worry about it. Some nurses are just a little temperamental at times. I just wanted you to know that I've been missing you. It doesn't seem possible that we just spent that one evening together because I feel like I've known you for ages. When do you suppose we could go on a real date? Do you have a day off this week?"

"Since this is a whole new experience for me, I'll admit I'm ready for some rest. I'm scheduled for the 3 to 11 shift tomorrow and Tuesday and then I'll have two days off."

"Hey, that's great. I'll have Wednesday off and maybe I can arrange my schedule to get Thursday off, too, if you'd like to spend them with me. Maybe we could drive out to the Garden of the Gods, Miramont Castle, or Bear Creek Nature Center. I've heard a lot about them and they all sound interesting. I haven't been to any of them yet, but if you have and would rather go someplace else, I'd be game to go anywhere you'd like to go. And, as usual, I'm probably pushing a little too hard here. I'm sorry, Monica, do you have other plans or things you need to do on your days off? I'd be willing to help if I can, like in the barn so I could be around the horses."

He could hear her giggling and he began to feel very foolish again. "Now, what have I done to embarrass myself?"

"Oh, Dan, you haven't done anything foolish." She paused for a moment and then let out a sigh before she continued. "I'm just amused at how hard you're trying to make plans to please me when I sense you'd be happiest just being out around the horses."

"Whoa, that isn't true at all, Monica, and I'm really hurt that you'd think I could be so uncouth. I like the horses, but you're the one that I really want to get to know."

"OK, I'm sorry, but I really need to go to the Landscape Pottery this week. I'd love to show you all of those places you mentioned, and the pottery is actually on the way to the others, but I don't think we can see all of them in one day."

He could hear her laughing softly. "I was just making suggestions. I'd love to go to the pottery or to a cold, dark cave as long as I'm with you. Can I take it, then, that we have a date starting early on Wednesday morning and maybe lasting through Thursday?"

"I think there may be a few details that'll need to be worked out there, Dan, but I'll agree to a date beginning Wednesday morning."

"You have made my day, Monica Reynolds, but I guess I'd better get some sleep so I can perform surgery in the morning. You'll never know how much this means to me. You're a sweetheart, and I hope you sleep well, too. Goodnight."

"Goodnight, Dan." As she hung up the phone, her thoughts were spinning around and around in her head. *How can I possibly want to spend time with this man who I have known for only a few days? Why couldn't I have just told him I had other plans instead of inviting him to go to the pottery with me? I never expected or wanted to really fall in love again after losing Terry, so what am I doing being completely swayed by a doctor who is probably just wanting to have some fun on his days off and finding me gullible to his charms. Calling me a sweetheart is most likely what he calls all the girls. Oh, Monica, what have you done now?*

She was startled by the phone ringing again, but this time it was Charlotte wanting to know why her phone had been busy for the last fifteen minutes. "Should I tell you the truth or just a little white lie? Of course, you know I can't tell you a lie, my friend, but you'll have to keep my secret because it could ruin the rest of my life if it got out. Will you promise you won't tell anyone, even your lovable Clint?"

"Oh, this sounds so exciting. Yes, I promise I'll zip my lips even to Clint although it will be extremely hard. You know we don't keep secrets from each other."

"Then I shouldn't ask you to do that, Char, because to cause a problem between you and Clint is the last thing I'd want to happen. Do you think he'll keep the secret if you ask him to?"

"He would be the last person on earth who would tell something that he has been asked to keep quiet about. Please, Monica, tell me before I explode!"

So Monica told her about her first day at work, meeting Dr. Wilder and about all the events happening since then. She then asked if she thought she'd been too eager tonight."

"Absolutely not, Monica. I wouldn't think that Dr. Dan Wilder, from what I've heard about him since he came here three years ago, would go out of his way to do anything with anybody socially. He has pretty much kept to himself, performed his surgery, and quickly disappeared into his small leased apartment. So, if you've brought him out of his shell and he is asking you to have a date with him, I'd consider it a genuine act of interest on his part. Oh, Monica, he isn't bad looking at all, and I hear that all the nurses swoon each time he goes by their station, a nurse by the name of Angela, especially. Have you met her?"

"Angela? Are you sure? Yes, I've met her. She has worked the same shift as I have the last five days. In fact, the last two she's been complaining that she's not feeling well, so I've been checking some of her patients as well as my own."

"Oh, I can see jealousy sprouting in those pretty green eyes. You'd better watch your back, Monica, because I've heard that she can be very sneaky when she puts her mind to it."

"How do you know so much about her, Char? She isn't a friend of yours, is she?"

"Heavens, No! I know who she is because she has an account at the bank. One of the tellers was saying Friday that a nurse by the name of Angela was telling the person she was with, while she was making a deposit, that there was a certain doctor she was going to reel in by getting a transfer. She also mentioned that a new nurse, who was making goo goo eyes at him, had better keep out of her way. I'd never made the connection until now, Monica, so I don't know what to tell you, but were you making goo goo eyes at him?" she laughed.

"Yea, really. As I just told you, I was running the other way as fast as I could go until he pulled into my driveway and I couldn't get away. Dan told me tonight, though, that he'd heard that Angela was requesting a transfer to the ICU, so maybe I won't have to work with her much longer. I'll be extra careful not to mention his name at the hospital, and especially at the station. Trudy, Ann, and Nancy have all been such good friends to me, but I won't talk to them about Dan either until I'm sure what Angela is going to do."

"That's probably wise until Angela at least gets her transfer. She's probably doing it so she can be closer to him. In a way, I hope she doesn't get it, but I'm also glad she won't be around to harass you. Now, back to the reason I called, when can we get together for lunch?"

"Tomorrow or Tuesday would be great for me. I don't go to work until 3 o'clock, so how does that fit your schedule?"

"Believe it or not, tomorrow would be wonderful. Why don't you drop by the bank at noon, and I'll join you as soon as I can get away. I'm so looking forward to seeing you, My Friend. It seems like ages since we've had a chance to talk."

"It really does. Until tomorrow, then. Thanks for calling, Char. Goodnight."

CHAPTER SIX

Monica wasn't surprised when she saw Dan pull into the drive about 6:30 Wednesday morning since he had called her Tuesday, during his lunch hour, to see if it would be all right to get there early. He had casually suggested that they might take an early morning ride before they headed to the Pottery. She smiles now as she is still wondering if it isn't the two horses that he is most interested in, but she would never again accuse him of that. She keenly remembers how upset he'd been with her the other day when she'd mentioned that could be a possibility.

She went to unlock the door of the sun porch and found him already there, waiting to come in. He had that rather embarrassed grin on his face again that she had become sort of used to in the few days they've known each other, but she held the door tightly closed for a minute indicating he couldn't come in. He was getting down on his knees to plead when she quickly opened the door.

"You must've gotten up with the chickens this morning, Dan, to get out here so early. Are you just itching to get on those horses and go for a ride in this lovely morning coolness?"

"I'm itching to do something, but it isn't necessarily to ride horses. Closing the door behind him, he smiled and asked, "Could I kiss you, Monica? Please? I've waited, although not very patiently, since last Wednesday when my pager had to spoil my chances of ending the evening so beautifully."

A little hesitantly, she put her arms around his neck and whispered, "I think I might be ready to start living again, Dan, and it would be nice to start this morning with a kiss."

Very tenderly, he wrapped one arm around her and drew her to him. He tilted her chin with his other hand and gently, so gently, placed his lips on hers. His arms joined each other on her back and pulled her closer until their bodies were pressed fairly close together. She wasn't sure she was ready for this much closeness, but it felt so good to be held by some-one again that she didn't object.

After kissing her several times, Dan took a step back and just looked at her with his blue eyes sparkling. "You are the most beautiful woman I have ever known, Monica. My life has taken on a whole new meaning since I met you, and I hope you enjoy being with me as much as I enjoy being with you. However," he grinned, "may I be so bold as to ask if you have any coffee made? I was in such a hurry to get out here, I didn't take time to fix any."

She couldn't help laughing. "You are so funny, Dan. You remind me of my first date, back when I was a teenager. It was his first date, too, and he was so eager to please. He'd start to say something, but then he'd forget what he wanted to say. When he finally did say something, he would just blush, grin, and squirm. You're not bashful, but you remind me of someone who's so eager and excited about a new discovery that he can't sit still."

"That describes me perfectly, but I hope I'm not acting like a teenager. To tell you the truth, though, I've dated very little so you may have to coach me along the way. Those few kisses were the first I've had in several years. Will you be willing to be my coach, Mauni?"

"If those were your first kisses in several years, Dan, I must say you haven't lost your touch. You probably need very little coaching. But, Mauni? Where did that come from?"

"I'm sorry. It just slipped out. Sometimes it just seems more loving to shorten names. In my dreams, I've found myself calling you Mauni, so I thought I'd try it out on you. If you don't like it, I'll never call you that again."

"I do like it, Dan. It just took me by surprise, that's

all. No one has ever tried to give me a nickname before. It is really unusual and also special because it came from you."

She had poured two cups of coffee and set them on the table. She went to the oven and removed a quiche, which she quickly dished up and placed a serving in front of him. She then sat down and held out her hand. He knew what to do with it this time, so he held it as gently as he could as he listened to her prayer.

Their ride was so refreshing in the morning stillness and not yet reaching the middle 80's predicted for later in the day. Monica loved telling the story about how the woods had become a part of their acreage, and Dan was all ears. "The trail had been cut into the woods and around the pond, all of which the owner insisted remain as an untouched woodland. It was to separate this land from several houses that were to be built on the other parcels of land he'd sold to pay his gambling debts, but he'd refused to sell this area.

However, when he put the house and the last ten acres on the market, there was a stipulation that had to be agreed to about the woods. He was really impressed with Terry's plan for a nursery and greenhouse, and after we'd expressed a love for the woods, he actually included that area in our deed, free of charge. Part of the deal, however, was his option to be able to come here and walk in the woods. He does come back occasionally to walk for hours in the woods, sit beside the pond, and talk to the animals who really seem to know him."

Dan pulled Tumbleweed to a halt so he could take in everything around him. He saw how the trees provided shade and a beauty that about took his breath away. They had ridden almost an hour when they stopped to rest at the small pond. Monica had a thermos of iced tea and some cookies which they enjoyed while the horses were enjoying a cool drink, too.

Monica had walked to the pond, removed her riding boots and dipped her toes into the water. It was so refreshing, she'd taken two more steps before she stepped on a slippery rock and found herself losing her balance. She let out a yell and went tumbling backwards with a big splash. Dan was there immediately to save her from drowning, so he thought, but she was laughing so hard, he could only join in. Finally, she reached out her hand for help to get back onto the dry grass, but she was quite a mess---wet and covered with sand. Rascal and Tumbleweed even added a whinny as they watched.

"Will Rascal mind if you ride in that messy condition?" Dan snickered, and he just continued chuckling until she filled her boot with water and came toward him with the intent of giving him a little shower, too. "Please don't do it, Mauni, because I don't have a change of clothes with me. We'll never get to the Pottery if you have to wash and dry my clothes while I sit in the nude. That might be fun, though, if you're going to wash and dry yours, too. Is that your plan?" His grin was priceless as he watched for her reaction to that remark.

She stopped short with the boot still in her hand. "You're very lucky, Dr. Wilder, that I want to go to the pottery, because you were going to get this water thrown on you and also pulled into the pond. You and your wet clothes would've dried in the sun, however."

"Gee, I thought you were a gracious hostess, but I'm beginning to see that devilish look in those eyes of yours. Should we be getting back so you can clean up and we can be on our way? The day will be gone before we know it, although I would be very content to stay right here, even if you did throw water on me."

"Maybe another day. Come on, get on your horse and let's go. I really do want to go to the pottery today." She was on Rascal quickly and off toward the meadow. He was elated that riding had come easily and naturally for him as he mounted Tumbleweed and caught up with her rather quickly. She'd then slowed the gait considerably, as they'd exited the woods, and Dan soon realized it was because the difference in the temperature was very noticeable. He was sure it was going to be a very hot day and the air conditioner in the car would most likely be much better than the top being down on a day like this.

After Monica had showered and put on clean clothes, she suggested that they take her small van because the items she wanted to buy might not fit in his car. He wondered if she would insist on driving, too, but she climbed in the passenger seat and waited for him to get in on the driver's side. They were on their way.

The day turned out to be perfect. Clouds had accumulated and blocked the sun most of the day so it didn't get as hot as had been expected. The pottery was busy, but Monica was successful in finding the items she'd wanted for the yard. She then suggested that they drive to the Garden of the Gods to have a picnic in the park. She'd surprised him again by packing a light delicious lunch, and he could hardly keep from hugging and kissing her for being so thoughtful.

They had toured the Visitor's Center and then decided to go to a movie where it would be cool and they could relax. He held her hand for awhile, but she'd wanted some popcorn so he put his arm around her shoulders while she munched. He was trying to watch the movie, but she was more appealing and he found himself watching her instead. He also leaned over and kissed the top of her head, and when she looked up at him, he then took the opportunity to kiss her lips. In the light of the screen, he could see that she was blushing but also smiling. *She is such an unspoiled beauty,* he mused.

When they finally exited the movie, they were surprised that it was almost 7:30 and so he suggested they find a nice restaurant for dinner to finish their first date in style. They were both in the mood for steak and found a restaurant to satisfy their appetites. Talk came easily as they discussed the day, all they had done, and how much they had enjoyed it. On the way to her house, the heat of the day had abated and he wished they had his car now, with the top down and the wind blowing through their hair. He was content, however, just to have her by his side.

He still wasn't sure what it all meant. These feelings were happening far too fast, not at all like his usual reactions after a week of knowing or dating someone. Of course, he had to grin at that thought when he remembered the number of dates he'd had in the last ten years. He was sure he could probably count them on the fingers of his two hands and maybe just a few toes. Most of them had been blind dates, set up by friends for a special occasion, and he had never asked for a second date. He had just preferred to stay home and dream of Christy. *Oh, Man, I thought I really had a crush on that little gal, so how can these feelings possibly be the real thing? Please, God, I want you to have full control over my life, but if this is the woman you have picked for me, I couldn't be more pleased.*

When he'd stopped in her driveway, he'd jumped out and raced around to open the car door. He pulled her into his arms, lifted her chin, and kissed her more passionately than he had intended. She gasped, as she tried to get her breath, and then whispered, "My, that was some kiss, Dr. Wilder. I think you may have had more experience than you want people to know."

"It must just come naturally," he chuckled, "but I'm glad you liked it, and there could be a lot more, just like that one, waiting for you, Mauni. I am more than ready to oblige at anytime, anyplace. But, am I going to be offered something to drink now," as he raised his eyebrows in question, "or are you going to send me home with parched lips?"

Laughing, she took his hand and they headed for the house. They'd decided to have some coffee since the air had cooled down and the wind was getting a little breezy.

CHAPTER SEVEN

While the coffee was brewing, they sat on the sun porch completely fascinated with the number of stars now twinkling in the sky. The clouds that had obscured the sun all day seemed to have vanished except for one or two fairly dark ones over in the west. The moon was big and bright and lit the yard in heavenly splendor. Dan reached his arm around her shoulders and pulled her to him.

"I feel so extremely blessed tonight, Mauni, for getting to share this day with you and I'm wondering if we could top it tomorrow. What do you think? Shall we try to think of a few things to do that'll even outdo today?"

"I'm sorry, Dan, but I do have some things I need to get done in the yard tomorrow or it'll get way out of hand. If you want to come out tomorrow afternoon, we could possibly do something in the evening. There's a nice restaurant not far from here that has a fantastic dance floor. They have a DJ and sometimes a live band there most weekends, but the juke box is playing the other nights. I've never asked, but do you like to dance?"

"Of course I like to dance. I even took ballroom dancing lessons for awhile during my hectic medical studies. There were four of us who decided we had to have something in our lives besides the books, so we signed up for six weeks of dancing. It was fun, but we got behind on our medical studies and had to really cram before the finals.

But, Ms. Monica Reynolds, I don't want to wait until tomorrow afternoon to see you again. In fact, I think I should stay here tonight so I can help you in the yard early in the morning, we could take another horseback ride, and then we can go dancing tomorrow night. Don't you have a couch I could crash on tonight? Pretty please, I don't want to drive clear home tonight and then back tomorrow. You know that song that says something like since I've found you, my arms are wrapped around you? Well, I don't want to be away from you, so if you won't let me sleep on your couch, I'll just sleep in my car."

"Dan, you're impossible! How would it look if you stayed here all night? The gossip would run rampant with that story. We'd better drink our coffee while you get your head on straight. You don't want rumors circulating any more than I do." She hurried off to get the coffee, but he was following her into the kitchen.

"I'm sorry if I upset you. I can understand your concern, but it is so isolated out here, I didn't think there'd be a chance of anyone finding out. I guess I really am, as you stated this morning, just too excited about my new discovery. I've finally realized I can actually have exciting, romantic feelings for a woman, and I don't want to miss a moment of my brand new adventure."

Monica set the cups of coffee on the table and slipped into her chair. She reached out her hand and he grasped it. "Dear Jesus, our ever loving Savior and Heavenly Father, it has been a wonderful day that you have given to Dan and me. It is getting late now, and I hate to have him drive home tonight and then back tomorrow, but I'm so uncertain what I should do. Please guide me to make the right decision. Amen."

She looked troubled, as they drank the coffee, and he smiled. "It's all right, Mauni, you don't have to feel as if you're doing something wrong. I probably shouldn't have asked, and I'll head home as soon as I finish my coffee."

They suddenly heard a rumble in the distance and realized it was thunder and a storm was definitely coming. "Where did all those stars and that beautiful moon go?" Dan asked as he went to check the sky. "Do you remember if we put all the car windows up?"

"I'm not sure. We didn't even unload my things from the pottery."

"That's right. We came in to have the coffee. I think I'll dash out and check to be sure," he said as he headed for the door. He couldn't believe the change in such a short time. It was really looking bad and the wind was getting a lot stronger, so he decided he would put the cars inside the garage. Luckily, he still had the keys to her car, from driving it today, but by the time he'd returned to the house, lightning was streaking across the sky and the thunder was closer and louder. It wasn't long until the rain started beating against the windows, which sounded like some hail might also be mixed in. The lightning was also flashing almost every minute, or so it seemed.

All of a sudden, a horrifying crack was just outside the house and a huge ball of fire erupted as a tree came crashing down just as the lights went out. Monica was in Dan's arms, shaking uncontrollably. She was whimpering as she said, "What if I'd made you go home, Dan, and you'd been caught in this? I would've never forgiven myself." But he then heard a little giggle as she said, "But, Lord, you really didn't need to be quite so demonstrative to get your point across."

She quickly found two or three large candles to light, and the battery-powered lantern hanging in the sun porch gave off a soft romantic glow. They had been able to see, with the many lightening flashes, that the tree which was hit had been on the opposite side of the road, but it had fallen across the road and had them blocked in.

Dan suddenly got up from the living room couch, where they had gone to get away from the windows in the sun porch, and asked, "Mauni, what about the horses? Do they get restless in a storm like this?"

"I don't think so. Terry usually went out to check on them, but he always came back in saying that they were OK. We haven't had a storm like this since he left."

"Do you have a raincoat that I could borrow? I'm going out to check on those horses. I can't sit here wondering if they're frightened and could possibly hurt themselves. Is there a right way to calm them?"

"I'll come with you. The raincoats are in the closet over here by the door. Can you see or feel your way toward the sun porch while I grab the coats and put out the candles?"

Dan had grabbed the lantern in the sun porch on their way out of the house so they could make their way to the barn safely although Dan had worried about Monica being out in this weather. The hail had stopped, but the lightening, thunder, and rain were still causing quite a commotion.

When they approached the barn door, they could hear the whinnies of Rascal and Tumbleweed and knew they needed solacing. Both horses were pacing in their stalls and Dan and Monica could see the fright in their eyes. Dan started talking softly, trying to calm them, while Monica found the other battery-powered lanterns and got them turned on.

It took only a few minutes to actually settle the horses down, but Dan wasn't going to leave them until the storm was over. He suggested that they spread some clean straw in one corner of the barn and lay down to get some rest. Monica found some blankets in the tack room and spread them on the straw. They were large enough to give some cover, too. Dan pulled her close to him so she could rest her head on his shoulder. He'd made a pillow for his head out of straw which he also covered with one of the blankets. When he knew she was asleep, he closed his eyes and sleep soon followed.

When he awoke, it was daylight, but Monica was still asleep with her head snuggled in the crook of his shoulder. He glanced at the horses and had to chuckle as they were both quietly watching them.

The storm was past and the sun had risen and was shining through the windows. He checked his watch and realized it was after 6:30 and most likely the horses were expecting something to eat. He didn't want to disturb Monica, though, because she probably needed the rest. She'd had all this responsibility on her shoulders for quite a while now, and he could imagine how it could wear anyone down without some help. Well, he intended to make sure she had help from now on. He continued to lie there, relishing the fact that she was in his arms and had felt comfortable enough to sleep beside him last night even if it was in a barn and somewhat a necessity.

In a few minutes, she stirred and then looked surprised when she realized her head was still resting on him. She sat up quickly as the horses whinnied and shook their heads. "This is probably quite a sight for them to see so early in the morning," she giggled. She picked up two pieces of straw to tuck in her hair as she stood up and walked over to the two stalls. Each horse took a piece of straw from her hair and she gave them a hug.

"Have you had a chance to check the damage?" she asked as she stroked the horses and then turned back around to look at him. "Oh, of course you haven't with my head on your shoulder. What in the world was I thinking? Thank you so much, Dan, for thinking about the horses and then insisting on sleeping here in the barn on a bed of straw. I slept better than I have in a long time."

She realized what she had implied and she knew her face was turning red when Dan reached her, pulled her into his arms and said, "Anytime you need a place to lay your head, Sweetheart, I'm available."

They worked together to feed the horses and put clean straw in their stalls. The water was checked and then they headed to the house to feed themselves. Monica realized she had left one candle burning when they had rushed off to the barn, but it had been in a deep safe container and the candle had just burned down and gone out. Since the lights were still out, they settled for cold cereal, orange juice, and a bagel.

Dan went out to see if the fallen tree had done any damage other than blocking the road. It had missed the white fence surrounding the yard by about 18 inches and he gave a thumbs up to God for that. He wasn't sure how they were going to get out yet, but he was going to call and see when the county maintenance could possibly move the fairly large tree.

He smiled as he stopped and opened the trunk of his car and pulled out a change of clothes. *Well, all right, so I fibbed a little when I stopped her from throwing water on me yesterday. At least, this way, I have clean clothes to put on after sleeping in the ones I wore all day and all night yesterday. God must have known I would need them because I'd thrown them in the trunk without much thought.*

Monica was anxious to hear about any damage, but then she saw the clothes he was carrying. "Dan Wilder, you lied to me yesterday about not having a change of clothes." She started laughing as she grabbed a dish towel and was going to snap him with it, but he was too quick. He caught her in his arms and gave her a long, loving kiss instead. She pointed to the bathroom and he hurried off to take a shower and get into his clean clothes. He'd noticed that she had accomplished that while he had been outside. *She'd looked so refreshed and so loveable, I just wish I could make love to her all day, and we don't need electricity for that. Whoa, where is that coming from? Maybe I'd better take a cold shower.*

He felt like a new man when he returned to the kitchen and found her busy making a casserole and some sandwiches. "If the lights come back on, I can bake the casserole, but if not, we'll be eating sandwiches, chips, and some fruit," she'd informed him without turning around. She slipped the sandwiches in plastic bags and quickly put them and the casserole in the fridge to try to conserve all the cold she could until the electricity came back on.

∽

Later in the morning, Dan was getting ready to suggest that they go into town for lunch when he suddenly remembered they were stranded here until that tree was moved. Not that he minded, but he hated that it was causing her more work because of him being here. "I realize I'm going to have a lot to make up to you, Sweetheart, when we get out of here, but are you still terribly concerned about the gossip?" He pulled her into his arms and gave her a little kiss. "I'm really sorry--well--not really," he chuckled, "that I was forced to stay here last night because of the weather, but you'd made it quite clear that you wanted me to go home."

He walked over to where she was now putting a small percolator on the gas stove to make coffee. She had finally found it almost hidden back in the small pantry. Being behind her, he put one arm around her waist, lifted her long hair up in the back with his other hand and kissed the nape of her neck.

She then turned to face him, her eyes brimming with tears. Putting her arms around his neck, she whispered, "Dan, I don't know what I would've done without you last night. I feel that God answered my prayer loud and clear, so I'm not going to worry anymore about rumors or gossip. If He wanted you here last night to console me, take care of the horses, and give me the best night's sleep I've had since Terry left for overseas, I'm ready to face whatever the future brings." She slowly brought her hand around from the back of his neck and patted his cheek gently, but then she turned back to her work.

CHAPTER EIGHT

Thank goodness for cell phones. About 4 o'clock Monica had used Dan's phone to call in and check her schedule for Friday. She found that she was still on the 3 to 11 shift through Saturday. Since the storm had kept her from working in the yard this morning, she now planned to spend Friday morning doing the things she had to get done there.

The maintenance crew had come around 1 o'clock to move the tree off the road, and the electricity had been restored shortly after that. Everything seemed to be back to normal except the phone. Dan had driven home to change clothes so they can go to the restaurant for dinner and also discover if they can dance together or not. She is still just a little concerned, since he'd told her he had taken lessons, whether she would be good enough to dance with him. She had always loved to dance and had done a lot during her teen years, and then she and Terry had danced quite a bit, too. She would probably feel a little anxious until she'd learned Dan's professionally taught technique.

He got back around 6:30 and they decided they were both rather hungry, so they took off for the Lazy Man's Bar and Restaurant. It was in a building which appeared to have come from a western ghost town with swinging doors into the bar, the high stools which were full, as well as other men standing at the bar. They were chatting or waiting for their drinks to take to one of the random tables scattered around the room.

Dan was a little surprised that Monica would want to come to such a place, but she proceeded straight through the bar and entered another room that proved to be a large rustic Early American restaurant which made you feel as if you'd stepped into another era. It had been beautifully decorated, and the tables were all covered with white tablecloths set with pewter plates, cloth napkins, and nice silverware. Crystal wine and water goblets were, of course, waiting to be filled. Etched hurricane globes enclosed candles on pewter bases, and they served as the center-pieces on each table.

Glancing around the room and admiring the Early American furnishings, Dan noticed the dance floor and juke box where soft music was playing, perfect for holding your lovely sweetheart and moving around the floor. He wanted to head that way instead of following the maitre d'. No one was dancing, but there were several couples eating which he expected to soon take advantage of the opportunity. Their table was not far from the dance floor, but not so close as to disturb their conversation.

Monica was giving him that 'fooled ya' didn't I' look and grin when they were seated, and without her uttering a word, he said, "Yes, Mauni, you definitely surprised me with this one. I was beginning to think I didn't know you at all when we walked into the bar. How did you and Terry ever find this place?"

"It was actually the man we bought the acreage from who told Terry about it. He'd said when it first opened about 15 years ago, it was going to be a bar and gambling casino, but they apparently didn't follow the rules so were ordered to close. Two families then went together and bought the building and thought it would be something a little unusual to keep the saloon style bar but have a very unique restaurant along with it. They have no menus so you never know if you'll be having steak, ham, pork, fish or chicken, to name a few, but they include a shellfish entree every Friday night. They have done very well and it is almost full every night of the week. We're a little early but it will be filling up before long."

"Can we dance while we're waiting to be served?"

"Certainly, but are you sure you want to see if I can follow you without making a fool of myself?"

They were on the dance floor dancing to the second song when they noticed that the server had brought their appetizers. The entire evening was one of the greatest Dan had ever had, and he knew his dancing partner had been the best possible. Not once did they step on each other's toes, so what more could he ask for except a wonderful kiss to say goodnight.

The nurses' station seemed a bit quiet when Monica arrived Friday afternoon. Trudy was checking in, but Ann and Nancy had worked days. A new nurse was on duty and it made her wonder if Angela had gotten the transfer she'd asked for, but she didn't mention it because Dan had been the one to tell her about it. No way did she want to explain how she knew about that bit of gossip. She walked over and extended her hand to the one she didn't know. "I'm Monica," she said with a smile, "I don't believe we've met."

"It's nice to meet you, Monica. I'm Sadie. I've worked in Maternity for years, but I guess I got the opportunity to come here so Angela could see what another ward was like. I worked with Trudy and Angela for a while yesterday, and with Ann and Nancy today. So far I think

I'm going to like it here. I work odd hours, though, so I'll be leaving around five."

"You'll like it a lot better, Sadie, when you get to work with Monica, I assure you." Trudy inserted into the conversation.

After Sadie had checked out, Trudy looked up from the papers she was checking and smiled at Monica. "I'm sure glad it's you I get to work with tonight. Angela was an absolute bitch last night. She'd apparently put in for a transfer to ICU but got switched to Maternity Ward instead." Not being able to keep from laughing, she heartily gave Monica the details of Angela's rage last night and explained that she now has to report to her new post at 6 a.m. in the morning. "No doubt about it, she was really one mad individual."

"I'm sorry she's upset. I would love to work the Maternity Ward myself. Of course, I'd rather be there as a patient," she smiled as she proceeded to check the patient list and to ask Trudy what she'd like her to do. "I'm all rested and ready to take care of the sick. It's so nice to be back doing the things I was trained to do."

"You're such a joy to work with, Monica, and I really missed you the past two days. So, you had a relaxing time, huh?"

"Yes, I had some work to do in the yard, and I needed some things from the Pottery, so I made a trip there and didn't even get the pots out of the car because of the storm. That was really something, wasn't it?"

"It was strange, because they reported that it only hit up around your area. We didn't get any hail or wind, and just a small amount of rain. Did you get some damage?"

"A tree was struck by lightning and fell clear across the road so we were pinned in until about 2 o'clock yesterday afternoon. The electricity was off, the horses were frightened, and I was absolutely terrified."

"You said 'we' so did you have someone with you, Monica?" She was grinning and had a questioning look in her eyes.

"Ah--just me and the horses. Why the big grin, anyway?"

"Oh--nothing, really, except Dr. Wilder was gone both days, too, and he never misses dropping by at least once when he has a day off. This was the first time in the last three years that he has taken two days off together. So, I was just wondering."

Monica could feel her face getting hot and redder by the minute, and she didn't know what to do about it. She could only think to herself. *Why was an innocent date suddenly turning into a nightmare? I should've known better than to let him come to the farm.*

"I'm sorry, Monica. I shouldn't have said anything, but I'm afraid your blushing face has given you away.

I don't think Nancy suspects anything, or maybe she doesn't feel it's any of her business, but Ann and I get very suspicious when things are not normal around here." Patting her on the arm, she continued, "I'll keep your secret, but with just the two of us here tonight, I hope to get some juicy details before 11 o'clock."

Monica hurried off to check in with her patients, but she heard Trudy giggling as she left. *Why didn't I just meet him in town or even better, not at all? Oh, Lord, what have I gotten myself into? I thought the storm was your sign for me to let him stay, and I would've been a nervous wreck if he hadn't been there with me, but what now? Do I confide in Trudy, as I did Charlotte, and hope things don't get any worse?* She very clearly heard the words from Proverbs 3:5-6, "Trust in the Lord with all your heart and lean not on your own under-standing; in all ways acknowledge Him, and He will make your paths straight."

With a lighter heart and a smile on her face, she entered the first room on her rounds. He was a teenager who had just turned 17. There had been a car accident late last night and he was suffering from a broken collarbone and a gash on his forehead. He was asleep when she entered, but he opened his eyes when she started to take his vitals. She smiled and told him her name, and then addressed him as Tyrone, which she had seen on his chart.

"From the extent of your injuries, it looks like you may have hit the windshield. Am I right?" she asked him.

"Yes, ma'am," he replied, "I was stupid and wasn't wearing a seatbelt. I understand my dad's remark now that young people think they're immune and that nothing can happen to them. I certainly know better after last night, and I'm paying a price. I was looking forward to my senior year on the football team, and now I'll probably sit in the bleachers and watch."

"Well, I'm facing a little problem of my own, Tyrone, and on the way to your room God gave me a Bible verse that helped me realize that I have to put my faith in Him, and it might just help you, too. Would you like to hear it?"

"Sure, Monica. I've heard a lot of verses in Sunday School, and my mom likes to recite them, but I haven't been very good at memorizing many of them. I've been told there are verses that are supposed to be answers to your problems, but I'm not sure I can believe that, but what's the verse that helped you?"

She repeated the verse that had come to her as she had walked to his room, and his eyes told her that it was registering in his mind and heart. "I don't think I've ever heard that one, but it does make a promise, doesn't it?"

"Yes, it does, Tyrone. I just ask that you hold onto that promise and trust that God can perform miracles. It may not be exactly what *you* want, but let it be God's plan and it will turn out fine. I'd better get on to my next patient, but I'll check back with you later."

"I'll be looking forward to it."

Monica's heart was singing as she finished her rounds. All the patients were resting quite comfortably, and the supper trays would be coming soon. There is always at least one patient that complains about the food, and one who gripes because it didn't arrive when he thought it should. Such is the life of the hospital which is truly her dream come true.

"Psst....Monica....someone's coming down the hall. Are you still hiding from him?"

"Who's him?" she asked as she giggled and watched Dan stop at Trudy's desk. She could see, however, that he had his eyes glued on her.

"Trudy, I'm about to leave for the day and I need to talk to Monica about a patient I just visited. Could she have a 5 minute break, please?"

"Of course, Dr. Wilder. The supper trays will be coming any minute so she'll be free while the patients are eating." Smiling her 'I know something' smile, she looked at Monica and said, "Take a break, Sweetie, and see what the doctor wants to talk to you about." She could hardly keep from laughing as she hid her face in her reports.

Those two definitely have something going on, and I'm going to find out what it is before I go home tonight.

Leading her into the empty waiting room, Dan turned to face her. "I couldn't leave without seeing you, and I was wondering how the horses get fed when you have to work this shift. Could I, please, drive out there and feed them tonight? I don't have a single thing to do this evening." He couldn't keep from grinning as they chose two chairs in a far corner.

"Dan, you're not making it easy at all. Trudy is already suspicious because you were gone for two days without dropping by the hospital, which I now understand is very unusual. Plus, I apparently slipped up and said we instead of I, and she isn't going to accept my poor explanation that I meant the horses. She says she's going to get the truth from me before I can go home tonight. What am I going to do?"

"Tell her the truth and ask her to keep it confidential. Trudy will not betray a plea for silence. Or, if you want to stretch the truth a little and tell her you've captured my heart and we're getting married very, very soon, I'll confirm that." His devastating smile was enough to make her want to slap him.

"Be serious, Dr. Wilder, or I may just do that and see how you'd really feel about such an outrageous rumor. You'd probably just have me fired, though."

"I am serious, but I guess you need some more time to really digest my true feelings for you. For now, just tell Trudy that I invaded your privacy because I wanted to meet you."

"I guess that'll suffice. By the way, did you hear about Angela's transfer?"

"I heard she got assigned to the Maternity Ward and wasn't very happy about it."

"From what Trudy said, she was outraged."

He couldn't help chuckling as he remembered Angela's comments to him last Sunday afternoon. His request for her transfer to the Maternity Ward must've been accepted. "That's what you nurses get when you mess with hospital protocol." He picked up her hand and was kissing it as he said, "As for me, though, a marriage with you wouldn't have to be a rumor, Monica, and I'd be delighted to affirm the statement." With that bombshell, he calmly stood and suggested again that she just tell Trudy the truth.

Pulling her to her feet, he continued, "I'm going to feed your horses tonight and then sit and talk to them until I'm sure they know who I am. Oh, and I'd better talk to you about a patient since that was my excuse to see you. It appears you made quite a hit with Tyrone, the young man I had to operate on very early this morning. Actually, it was soon after I left you. When I saw him earlier, he was terribly upset about his condition and not being able to play football this Fall. His attitude was completely different just now. When I asked what had happened, he said a very nice nurse had given him a Bible verse and a whole new outlook on his future. It could only have been you."

"Tyrone seems like a great kid who has been exposed to Bible verses by his mother and in Sunday School. I think this accident opened his eyes and he just needed a little nudge to see that God has a plan for each of us. I'll see him later and maybe I can talk to him a little more."

"You're a wonderful addition to this floor, Mauni. Some of the patients are facing a real change in their lives because of their physical condition, and encouragement is the one thing they all need a lot of. You gave that to Tyrone, and I appreciate it immensely. I find it to be a good part of the healing process, too, when a patient has a relationship with God."

He very softly kissed her on the cheek. "I'd better go. I'll miss you until I can see you again, My Dear Lady." He then bowed and watched her return to the nurses' station before heading to the elevators. *She doesn't know it yet, but it's going to be a lot sooner than she thinks when we meet again.* A big smile was on his face as he watched the monitor click off the floors. He'd soon be on his way to the farm to make friends with two big, wonderful horses.

CHAPTER NINE

Monica was still thinking about her conversation with Trudy when she turned into her drive about 11:30. It had been a short talk because they'd been the only two on duty, but she had been so happy for her. Now, however, Monica's sort of surprised to see Dan's car still parked in front of the garage. *He'd said he was going to feed the horses, but surely he didn't mean to spend the whole night with them. Could something have happened or did he just decide to wait for me?*

She jumped out of the van and ran toward the barn. She could see a dim light shining through the small window and around the warped door that she kept forgetting to have fixed. She made a mental note to herself again, but right this minute her heart was pounding as she pushed the door open and looked around. She saw him, stretched out on the straw bed where they had slept two nights before. He wasn't moving so was he asleep or hurt?

She dashed to the spot and fell on her knees, whispering, "Dan, are you all right? Did something happen? Please talk to me."

With one quick move, he grabbed her and pulled her down beside him. "Gotcha," he laughed, and then covered her mouth with his. She responded hesitantly at first but then he drew a more passionate response as he deepened the kiss. She was keenly aware of the smell of straw as his lips moved to her hair, her cheek, and even nibbled her earlobe before going back to her mouth. After several of those intriguing kisses, she had to push away and sit up, almost gasping for breath. She turned and faced the horses while she spoke softly, trying to keep her voice steady. "Dan, we shouldn't be doing this, and why are you still here?"

He just chuckled as he reached his arms around her and pulled her back down against his chest. She could feel his heart beating as hard as her own, and she could so easily wish the moments they'd just shared could go on forever. She pulled away again, however, and sat completely up when he released his hold on her.

He'd sat up also and just looked at her while trying to determine if she was upset with him or just trying to gain control of her feelings. He had felt the pounding of her heart and the response to his kisses, but was she ready to admit she was in love with him?

He murmured, "Mauni, I would've had coffee made for you, but I didn't have a key to go in the house, and I also thought it might be too hot for coffee. Are you sorry I stayed, or do you want to go in and have something to drink with me now? Maybe you'd prefer that I just be on my way."

His voice sounded as if his feelings were hurt, and Monica realized that she might've been a little harsh when she'd asked why he was still here. "I'm sorry, Dan, if I sounded like I wasn't happy to see you, but it did surprise me that you stayed until I got home. You must've had a good long talk with Rascal and Tumbleweed. Let's go in and I'll see what I can fix for us to eat, because I'm starved."

She stood up and he was right beside her. "I just can't stay away from you, Mauni, so I made a decision tonight, and the horses agreed with me. Want to know what it was?"

"Well, if my horses agreed with it, I most certainly want to know what you three have decided. Tell me on the way to the house." She couldn't help but grin at his expression that was totally unreadable at the moment.

He tilted her chin and gently swept his lips across hers, and then with his arm around her waist, he escorted her to the door, made sure it was latched, and then they walked hand in hand toward the house. "Well, it's like this, Mauni. Rascal, Tumbleweed, and I like you so much that we think there should be no secrecy anymore about our relationship. Therefore, I have decided that, starting right now, I am *not* making any excuses if I want to see you at the hospital, and I may start wearing a tag saying I'M TAKEN. I'll make sure everyone knows where I am when I take one, two or three days off. We are going out on dates and even trips whenever we like. Will you agree with the decision of your three most ardent admirers?"

In a daze, Monica unlocked the door and made it into the kitchen. *I couldn't have heard him right. He's just teasing about talking to the horses, of course. It would certainly be wonderful, if it were true, but I can't let myself believe that he is serious.*

"You must've really had quite a conversation with Rascal and Tumbleweed to come up with a far-fetched decision like that. Everyone seems to know how you like to be alone when you're away from the hospital and that your apartment is your own secluded haven. Would you like some scrambled eggs and toast, or would you like me to make you a big hearty sandwich?"

Scrambled eggs sound great if you're fixing some for yourself. May I put some coffee on while you're fixing the other?"

"That would be great, Dan. You know where things are."

Dan was dumbfounded with her answer about his decision, but he decided to wait until they were eating to continue the discussion. *I'll admit I stayed pretty much to myself, but it was only because I didn't have someone I wanted to spend time with. That has all changed since I've met her, and now I have to convince her that my decision is real, it's what I want, and I'm not giving up until she wants it, too. I read a verse this morning from Isaiah, but can I remember all of it? It went something like- -'For I am the Lord, your God, who takes hold of your right hand and says to you, Do not fear, I will help you.' Well, I'm going to hold onto that promise, Lord, because I may face an obstacle here and need your help.*

He then noticed that Monica had set a plate of scrambled eggs and toast in front of him and was now pouring the coffee. "I'm sorry, Sweetheart, I should have done that, but I guess my thoughts had me forgetting my duties."

"Can you share your thoughts with me?" she asked as she sat down.

"I was just remembering a verse I read this morning saying that God will take hold of my right hand and help me. I think I'll hold Him to that promise."

"I've always liked part of a poem I read a long time ago which said, 'Prayer can move a mountain, if we trust that God knows best. Perhaps instead He'll give us strength to climb and meet the test.' Are you needing some help, Dan?"

"I'm not sure, Monica. It depends on how you decide to accept the decision that the horses and I made tonight." Chuckling, he continued, "I suppose it does sound a little far fetched, but I'm totally serious. I have never felt like this before toward anyone, and even though I haven't dated a lot, I do know the difference between friendship, infatuation, and true love. I'm truly in love with you, Monica, and I intend to do my best to earn your love in return."

"Dan, it is just so quick. It isn't a matter of friendship versus love, because the time we've spent together assures me that there is more than just friendship involved. It's more a need to learn a lot more about each other and not be embarrassed by the whole hospital staff watching our every move. I've just started working, and I certainly don't want to be a gossip item. I also can't take off every time you decide you'd like to go someplace. How would that go over with the other nurses? Can you understand where I'm coming from? I also have to think of Terry's parents even though they *have* been encouraging me to start a new life. I don't think they meant a whirlwind romance."

I guess I got carried away with my thoughts and dreams tonight, but I didn't mean to imply that we would flaunt our relationship. I was thinking more like being able to talk to you at the nurses' station, and possibly a lunch together now and then. Some days I'm in the OR from 7 a.m. to 7 or 8 p.m. and on those days I do like to go home and drop into my old comfortable recliner. I was also thinking we could learn more about each other as we date and spend time together, and you *will* get a vacation, you know, so maybe we could take a trip then."

"That makes it a little clearer, but I still feel it's a little soon to be making too many of these plans of yours. I guess I can go along with your decision for awhile and see how things work out." She got up and started clearing the table. "What is your schedule tomorrow? Do you have to make rounds early on Saturday mornings, or do you get to sleep in? It's getting pretty late, and I thought if you had to get to the hospital early in the morning, you'd better be going. If not, since I work afternoons again, you could sleep here and then drive home in the morning instead of fighting the Friday night wild and crazy drivers." She could feel her face getting hot and knew that Dan was noticing her blushing. "By that, I didn't mean we would sleep together, Dr. Wilder, but I do have a guest bedroom."

He couldn't keep from laughing at her as she tried to explain that she had no intention of sleeping with him, even like the other night in the barn. "Is your guest room in the barn on a bed of straw?" he chuckled, "or are you actually going to trust me to sleep in your house? You do remember, don't you, that I behaved myself the other night, although the horses were there as our expert chaperones?"

"You're impossible, Dan, and I should make you drive home. To be honest, though, I don't want you out there driving when it's so late and on a weekend."

"Are you trying to be my guardian angel, Mauni?" he chuckled.

"Well, guardian angel sounds better than an old mother hen. Come on, I'll show you where the guest room is. You didn't answer me about the hospital, though."

"I'll make rounds in the morning but it doesn't have to be real early. I also have one appointment at 10:30 with a man who couldn't get off work during the week. I've seen the reports that his physician sent over, and I'm afraid surgery is imminent. He'll also have to take time off to recuperate, so I need to fully explain the procedure to him. His doctor has already discussed it with him, but he is somewhat concerned that he'll try to postpone the surgery and risk losing his life."

When she had turned on the lights in the bedroom and explained that there was only the one bathroom, he smiled and put his hands at her waist. "You are the sweetest and most beautiful person I've ever met. Your blushing is adorable and I love you so much." He then put one arm around her, raised her chin with a soft touch of his finger and kissed her very tenderly. He immediately headed her toward the door. "Goodnight, Sweetheart."

She locked the doors and crawled into bed, hoping to fall asleep fast as she realized she was overly tired. Her thoughts, however, went back to Trudy, who had been so excited to hear that Dr. Wilder had found his match, and how optimistic she had made her feel. Not that she could honestly believe it, but it was nice to realize that Trudy was happy for her and not the least bit judgmental.

Could I possibly have a chance with Dr. Dan Wilder, the evasive bachelor who has all the nurses swooning every time he comes near? Could something this unbelievable mean that I'm so lucky that he would actually love me? He could have any woman he wanted, so why would he pick a widow, a rather poor widow at that?

Terry had had some insurance, and his folks had been quite generous while she was negotiating the settlements, but she is pretty dependent on her job now and the income from the investments she'd made. She has to consider how all of her actions might be regarded so not to jeopardize her income.

She had thought several times about the small apartment Char had told her Dan was renting, and how he had almost no social life. *Maybe God is reaching out to both of us to help us find a new happiness together. He is much more handsome now, his face has relaxed and there seems to be a constant smile, so I still can't believe he'd want to settle for me. He has been so helpful, such a gentleman, he loves my horses, he's considerate, funny, loving, handsome, smart, very handsome. . .* and that is the moment she fell asleep, smiling.

CHAPTER TEN

Monica awoke Saturday morning to the smell of coffee, glanced at the clock beside her bed and grimaced. It was almost 8 o'clock and she remembered that Dan had slept here last night. It had been after 1 o'clock when she'd gotten to bed, but she was always up by 6:30 to feed the horses and get the morning chores done.

She jumped out of bed, pulled on a pair of shorts and a T shirt, and then darted to the kitchen. Dan was just putting something in the oven and then he turned, gave her one of those devastating smiles, and started toward her. "You were definitely tired last night, Mauni, and I'm glad you could sleep a little later this morning.

I fed the horses, although they looked a little surprised to see me instead of you, and I have coffee ready." He had reached her and slipped his arm around her waist. "May I have a good morning kiss from my sweetheart?" He hadn't waited for her answer as his lips found hers, but she had immediately put her arms up around his neck.

"You'll make someone a great husband someday, Dr. Wilder," she remarked when he ended the kiss. "I've never had coffee ready for me before, and what am I smelling that is making my stomach growl like a hungry lion?"

"Oh, that's just a very simple coffee cake that my nanny taught me to make when I was about five years old. I found all the ingredients so I decided to show you that I'm not lost in a kitchen." That grin was something she could never get enough of.

"What time did you get up anyway? You didn't get to bed any earlier than I did, so why were you up so bright and early?"

"Think back, Darling. What was I doing when you got home last night? If I recall, I was asleep on our straw bed in the barn and had been for a couple of hours. The horses and I had finished our conversation, so I curled up and went to sleep. I'd had close to 2 hours sleep by the time you got home."

By the time the table was set, the orange juice was poured, and she'd had her first cup of coffee, the delightful cake was out of the oven and they sat down to eat. Her prayer this morning ended with "Thank You, God, for all the blessings You have given me since the 6th of July. Amen."

Could it have been only ten days? It seems as if Dan has been in my life forever, and it feels so comfortable having him there. Can I ever face the possibility now of losing him? It's still so hard to imagine that Dr. Dan Wilder had even looked at me, let along wanted to spend time with me. Well, I'm going to enjoy it while it lasts and let the future be in God's hands. If it is His plan, it will turn out just fine.

She looked over at Dan and realized she must've been daydreaming because he was frowning as he watched her. "I'm sorry," she giggled as she took a big bite of the coffee cake, "my thoughts must have wandered. I was thinking about all that has happened in the last ten days, and it seems so unbelievable."

"You're so right, Mauni. I can hardly comprehend that I've found someone who can make my heart pound like a jackhammer, who makes me sleep on a bed of straw and love it, one who lets me mess up her kitchen and just grins, and one who causes me to throw caution to the wind where my love life is concerned." Chuckling, he pushed his chair back and stood. "I love spending time with you, Sweetheart. However, you know I'd better be on my way so I can get cleaned up, get to the appointment on time, make my rounds, and hopefully get a chance to see you before you go on duty. Do you think you could manage to come early enough to do that?"

"If you were to insist, I suppose I could push myself

and get there about 2:15 so I can meet you in the cafeteria. Would that be OK? By the way, Charlotte and Clint want to come and ride late this afternoon, so they'll take care of the horses. They've done this quite a few times to give me a break, and also when Terry and I wanted to get away." She could see the disappointment in his eyes, so hurriedly continued, "Dan, I didn't ask them to do this. It's just that Charlotte called yesterday and asked if they could ride, not even knowing that I had to work the 3 to 11 shift. When she realized that, she then offered to schedule their ride later so they could do the feeding. Come here, give me a smile and a kiss before you scoot."

"Could I be here to welcome you home? Of course, I can't get in to have something ready for you to eat, but I could meet you at the hospital and then we could go some place and eat. Which would you like?"

"I'll probably be ready to come home and kick my shoes off, but I hate to have you drive way out here again."

"Hey, I love it out here, and I won't mind the drive when I know I'll get to see you when you get home. I'll just wait in the car until you get here."

"I'll give you the spare key, and you can come on in and relax. I'll have iced tea and lemonade made. It's supposed to be a scorcher again today, so coffee probably won't sound too good. If we want to change the plan, we can when we meet at 2:15. OK?"

"That's my girl, always thinking of a way to escape from me. Well, I'm not going to let you, Sweetheart, so I'll take that kiss and a key and get out of your hair for a few hours."

Monica had accomplished a lot after Dan left, and she was in great spirits when she had to leave for work. The house looked good, the yard looked good, and the barn had also been cleaned and aired.

Dan wasn't there when she arrived at the cafeteria at 2:10, so she got a soft drink and found a booth in the far corner. She thought he would be coming any minute, and from her vantage point she'd be able to see him come in the door. However, at 2:45 she had to leave and check in for work, but Dan still had not arrived. *What could have happened?* Her mind, of course, started running the gamut of reasons but only one crowded her thoughts. For some reason, he'd changed his mind about her and was ending their relationship without even an explanation. She tried to convince herself that there had to be another reason, but what could it be? She grabbed her purse and started to leave, but just then an intern hurried into the cafeteria and looked at her questioningly.

"Are you Monica?" he asked.

"Yes, I'm Monica. Is there anything wrong?" Her

thoughts were whirling around in her head like a wind storm. *Had something happened to Dan on his way home this morning?* Her throat was suddenly dry and she felt tears welling up in her eyes, but it then dawned on her. *Oh, Monica, how stupid of you not to realize that he was called for another emergency. After all, he is a surgeon,* she scolded herself quietly.

"No, not with Dr. Wilder," the young man answered, "but he's still in the OR doing a second emergency surgery. He'd just finished one emergency when another was admitted. It appears to be a difficult case, so he wanted me to tell you that he was so sorry that he couldn't meet you as planned. He will stop by the nurses' station before he leaves the hospital. Was there anything you'd wish to tell him?"

She smiled at the intern as she thought of so many words she would like to say to the talented and handsome Dr. Wilder, but she just shook her head and said, "Just tell him I'll talk to him a little later. And thank you for coming to tell me he couldn't meet me."

She'd noticed a subtle smile on his face as he turned and hurried out the door. *O.K., Danny Boy, it appears a bit of news about us is starting already and it's not at the nurses' station. I hope you're ready for the consequences.* She didn't know whether to laugh or cry as she headed for the elevator.

Ann was just arriving when Monica reached the station. She looked like she was about to burst with some news. "What has you so excited?" Monica asked as Ann took her hand and pulled her into the supply room.

"I just couldn't wait to tell you that Angela turned in her resignation yesterday and has taken a job at the Retirement Center in Denver. I don't know a lot, but we'll talk later. We'd better get the girls relieved now so they can go home."

Monica was shocked although happy, in a way, that Angela was going to be gone and wouldn't be there to make any more trouble. Charlotte had warned her that Angela could play dirty, and she'd heard a few of her remarks that had been quite cruel. She'd been very careful, although clever, not to use names, but it was obvious to whom they were intended. However, she's sorry the hospital is losing a good nurse, since nurses are hard to find these days.

It was almost 6 o'clock when Dan arrived at the station looking tired and disturbed. He asked if she would join him in one of the family waiting rooms and, without waiting for a reply, he walked away. She glanced toward Ann, who motioned for her to go, so she hurried to catch up to him and they entered the room together. "I'm sorry, Mauni," he said quickly as he placed his face in his hands and she could hear the sobbing and see his body reacting to his distress. She led him to a couch and urged him to sit down and talk to her.

"I lost him, Mauni. I lost a little boy who was just riding his bicycle on the sidewalk where he would be safe, and then...h-h-he was h-h-hit by a mo-tor-cy-cle turning into a dri-driveway. I tried so ha-hard; I did ev-every-th-thing I knew how to-to do to save him, but it-it wasn't e-enough." He continued to weep as Monica held him in her arms, just stroking his back and trying to console him.

This was a new experience for her, and she wondered if this had been his first loss. It confirmed the fact that there are so many things they still don't know about each other. Here she is, holding this giant of a man, so compassionate and caring, and as broken up as if it had been his own son. She loved him so much at this moment, realizing his need for real comfort, but also wondering if she was strong enough to give it.

He finally sat up, wiped his eyes, and just looked at her. She couldn't read his mind, so she was concerned that she had done something wrong. "Dan, are you really all right? I can imagine what you've been through and I'd like to help you, but I'm at a loss. I guess I'm too new at this nursing business."

He put his arm around her shoulders and pulled her to his side. "You were all I needed, Mauni, just you here beside me. A child is so precious, and to see one die right in front of your eyes, it is terribly hard to comprehend. I'd thought my day was finished when he was brought in, and I knew that it was bad. A whole team of doctors was trying to think of something else to try, but we'd exhausted our medical expertise. His little body was just so damaged.

Knowing that you cared was such a comfort. I just need to go home now and sort it all out. It was my first loss, and I'm just a bit confused, upset, and angry. I don't think I'd be very good company tonight, so, if you don't mind, I'm going to beg off meeting you later." He looked at her so sympathetically, as if he didn't really want to say that, but he also knew he needed to be by himself for a while.

"Dan," she started to say something but then stopped. "Never mind, I understand the reason that you need time alone."

"Come on, Monica, finish your thought. What were you going to say to me?"

"Oh, I was just going to ask if I could possibly stop by your apartment, when I get off work, and make sure you're OK before I go on home, but . . . . ."

"You would really do that for me? If you'll stop by, I'll tell you how to find it. You know it's only five blocks from the hospital, and it's not much out of your way when you're going home."

At 11:15 Monica parked in front of the building Dan had described to her. She could tell in the glow from the street lights that it was a well maintained building, and the yard was beautifully landscaped. She could see lights coming from one of the apartments and assumed that it was his. She'd changed into a bright yellow knit top with a pair of plaid crop pants of yellow, blue and white before leaving the hospital. Her dark hair and tanned skin was quite a contrast against the yellow of the shirt. She'd made it a habit to bring a change of clothes to work with her just in case there was an accident at the hospital. She didn't like driving home in soiled uniforms, and, at this moment, she was so glad she didn't have to look like a nurse.

When she'd reached the lobby, Dan was waiting for her. He'd quickly taken her hand in his and given it a squeeze which had felt so comforting. "It's been a long, rough evening," he whispered, "and I've been counting the minutes until I'd have you with me again." After entering the apartment, he wrapped his arms around her and gave her a rather emotional kiss that caused her a few tingling moments. It made her wonder if coming here had really been the best idea. She pushed away, gasping for breath. "Dan, let's sit down so we can talk."

CHAPTER ELEVEN

With one arm still around her, Dan tilted her chin up with his other hand so he could look into her eyes. Grinning, he kissed the tip of her nose and asked, "Did I get carried away a little there?" His lips had returned to hers before she could answer, but this time it was a nice short and gentle kiss. He reluctantly released her, when she again pushed on his chest, but he grabbed her hand and pulled her to the couch. "I just need to hold you, Mauni."

She finally got a chance to see the living room of his apartment, and she decided that it was definitely a man's pad. A very comfortable leather couch, in a rich brown sable, was along one wall with oak end tables and tall wooden lamps. A matching club chair was on one side of a large stone fireplace and a comfortable-looking beige recliner was on the other side. There were no pictures on the walls or tables, but she did notice that there were several books lying by the recliner. A bookcase was full of books to the right of the front windows, which had vertical blinds, and an entertainment center was just inside the door on the left side of the windows. The walls appeared to be painted a nice creamy tan that complemented the leather furniture. It was, she concluded, in its own manly way, very cozy and it was definitely not the small apartment Charlotte had her visualizing he was living in.

He'd pulled her back against his chest and had been, for several minutes, winding his fingers through her hair when she finally asked, "Dan, are you going to be all right so I can drive on home?" There was no answer, but he leaned down to nibble her earlobe, kiss her cheek, and was heading for her lips. She could hear him chuckling so she quickly moved out of reach. "Dan, I asked you a question. May I go on home and get some rest?"

"I don't want you driving out there tonight anymore than you wanted me to drive back home last night, so, why don't you stay here tonight? I'll get you up early in the morning, fix breakfast, and I'll even plan to go to church with you. I'll shower while you drive on home, feed the horses, and get cleaned up. Will that give you enough time to get to church?"

"I shouldn't do that, Dan. What if someone sees my car out in front? We'll be the talk of the town, or at least the hospital."

"I'll go out and put your car in my garage. I have two

bedrooms and two baths, so you'll have all the privacy you want." Chuckling, he got up and then pulled her up from the couch and again into his arms. After just a peck on the cheek, however, he took her hand and led her to the guest bedroom. It was a mansion compared to the little room she'd made him sleep in at her house. The walls were a soft green, and a very pretty colorful quilt was on a queen-sized bed. There was an oak dresser with mirror, and an upholstered chair in mauve sitting beside a table and lamp. It was very elegant.

"Would you like something to eat or drink before we hit the sack?" he ventured as he could tell she was definitely undecided about what to do. "Why don't you go and check the refrigerator to see if anything looks good to you while I go and move your car? May I have your keys?"

He'd watched as she looked at the room and then turned to look at him. "How did I get talked into this, Dan?"

"Because I needed you this afternoon and now you need to relax, eat something, and get a good night's sleep. Come on, Mauni, get your keys for me."

It hadn't taken him long to move her car, and then they'd decided to have just a little ice cream and some cookies before saying goodnight. He'd given her one of his tall t-shirts to sleep in, walked her to the bedroom door, enjoyed an arousing goodnight kiss, and then he had hurriedly gone to his room and closed the door. "I'm definitely in love," he whispered.

When Monica awoke the next morning, the bed felt so comfortable that she really did **not** want to get up, but then Dan knocked on her door and called her name. She then realized where she was, jumped out of bed, and headed for the bathroom. Looking in the mirror, she's rather surprised to see the glow of happiness in her eyes. *Is this guy for real?* She grins as she remembers the sweet goodnight kiss and all the kindnesses he has shown since they met only twelve days ago. She keeps thinking that she must be playing Cinderella at the ball, but she's afraid her coach will be turned back to a pumpkin any day. It doesn't seem possible that a fairy tale love affair could happen to her.

The smell of coffee and bacon drifting into the room has her stomach rumbling from starvation. She pulls on the clothes she'd been wearing last night, then gets her brush out of her purse and tries to tame her hair a little after the wonderful night's sleep. She'll have to be on her way home shortly or she won't be ready for church. The 23rd Psalm comes to her and she whispers, "Yes, the Lord is my Shepherd, and I shall not want because He leads me in the paths of righteousness."

She arrives in the small kitchen where Dan is at the

stove fixing the bacon and eggs. He turns and gives her a dazzling smile and then reaches out his arm for her to come to him. "I think I've seen that outfit somewhere before, Sweetheart, but it looks as good now as it did then." He kisses her lightly on the lips and then puts her to work fixing the toast.

She was soon on her way home, and she went directly to the barn to feed the horses, muck the stalls and add fresh hay. When she reached the house, she noticed she had at least two calls on her answering machine. *Should I take time to listen to them now or get ready for church? Dan will be coming soon and I don't want to be caught in the shower. The calls can wait. They're most likely telemarketers that I don't want to listen to anyway.* When she was in the shower, however, she worried who the calls were really from, when had they called, and what are they thinking? "Oh, Lord, what have I done now?" she moaned. Then, as she got out of the shower, she heard the phone start ringing. She quickly grabbed her robe and answered the one on her nightstand. "Hello," she said, but was surprised to hear Dan's voice.

"Mauni, I'm so sorry, but I just got a call for another emergency. A man by the name of Reynolds collapsed at his home, and they feel it might be his heart. Honey, could this be any relation to Terry? I believe his first name is Claude."

Monica almost dropped the phone as she gasped, "Oh, Dan, it's Terry's dad. Please do hurry and do the best you can for him. I'll be on my way as soon as I get dressed." She ran to the answering machine in the kitchen and pushed the button. The first call had been from Charlotte who just wanted to tell her that their ride had been great and she'd see her later in church. The second call was from Terry's mom. Thankfully she'd assumed that she was at the barn and went on to tell her that the ambulance had just now arrived to take Claude to the hospital. He'd felt faint and then had collapsed on the floor. She hoped that Monica could come to the hospital, and they were trying to get Dr. Wilder because she'd remembered her mentioning how good a heart doctor he was.

Monica quickly pulled some dress slacks and a top from the closet and was dressed in a jiffy. She grabbed her purse and was on her way. How she hated to miss church, but God would want her to put family first. She was praying as she drove toward the hospital asking for God's healing hand on Terry's dad and to give his mother the strength to handle the crisis. She asked for guidance and skill for Dan as he tries to save another life. She couldn't help but smile as she also thanked Him for watching over her by letting both of the phone calls be non-judgmental.

When she reached the waiting room on the surgical

floor, Terry's mother was pacing and crying softly. Monica went to her and took her in her arms. "Would you like to go to the chapel and pray?" she asked.

"Maybe a little later, Monica. I hope to hear something from the doctor or intern in a little bit. They said that someone would be out to talk to me before they start any surgery on him. I called Glenn, but it will be after lunch before he can get here. I'm so glad you could come, Sweetheart. You have been the daughter I never had, and you've always been there for us. I hated bothering you on Sunday, but I was sure you'd want to know."

"I'm so glad you did, Gladys. I'm sorry I wasn't in the house to answer your call. It must've been terrifying to see him fall and not know what caused it. I'm sure we'll have some answers soon." She led her mother-in-law over to some chairs and sat down. She was telling her about her job, how much she liked it, and how she'd really enjoyed her very first patient, Josh, when she sensed someone coming into the room. When she looked up, Dan was there and he was smiling.

"Good morning, Ladies. I'm Dr. Wilder and I'm very happy to tell you that Claude is going to be fine. It appears to have been a bad case of indigestion, which caused him to have some shortness of breath, and that, in turn, caused him to faint. We have him stabilized and we're going to admit him for 24 hours so we can monitor him and then give him instructions on diet, exercise, etc." He started out of the room but turned back. "There's a short service in the chapel on Sunday mornings, if you'd be interested. It'll be starting in about 15 minutes so I'm planning to attend since I'm not in OR. Would you like to join me? I have to quickly sign the admission papers, but I'll be back in about 5 minutes to get your answer." His eyes were twinkling as he glanced directly at Monica. He winked and then left the room.

"Oh, Monica, his is such a nice doctor and so handsome. Is he married or could there be a chance, well, you know? Claude and I would love for you to meet someone with whom you could find happiness again."

"Dr. Wilder and I *have* become friends in the last two weeks, but I don't know if he's wanting it to become more than just friendship. He certainly is handsome, and I love having him as a friend."

"Well, if I were you, I'd push for more than friendship, and I saw that wink. I know you've wanted to have a child or two, and the years do pass quickly, you know." Smiling, she gave Monica a hug and was wishing her a happy future just as Dan walked in the door.

"Are you ladies going to join me for a little preaching?" His smile included both of them, but it was Gladys who made the first move.

"Well, we certainly are, Dr. Wilder. We really need

to thank God for sending you to us this morning and for your quick diagnosis. I feel this is a day for everyone to enjoy the blessings of His love in their lives. I sure hope Monica can find happiness again soon," she sighed, "and I wish you lots of happiness, too, Dr. Wilder." She very discreetly moved to the other side of Monica so that Dan would be next to the one she'd noticed all of his smiles had been directed toward.

Dan, of course, was enjoying every little bit of whatever Gladys was trying to slyly accomplish. He wasn't sure what had been happening when he'd walked back into the room, but he'd heard Gladys wishing Monica a happy future. He was beginning to think she might be in his corner, so he took Monica's hand as they headed toward the chapel. He'd taken one more quick glance at Gladys which gave him confidence. She had a big smile on her face, but he didn't know that she was whispering a prayer, "I'm counting on you, Lord."

CHAPTER TWELVE

Monica stayed with Gladys until her son, Glenn, arrived shortly after they had eaten lunch in the cafeteria. They had visited with Claude, after the service in the chapel, and Dan had excused himself to make rounds. Gladys had asked him to join them for lunch, but he'd thought he had better not push his luck with Monica by exploiting this sweet lady's obvious desire to give Monica a happy future. He'd smile at Monica, when he'd gotten the chance, and mouthed that he would talk to her later.

Monica visited with Glenn for a few minutes in Claude's room, and then gave the patient and Gladys a big hug before leaving to find Dan. He was in his office reading some papers and talking to another doctor, but she didn't feel embarrassed since she was going to ask about Claude and make sure he had told Gladys everything. Dan noticed her right away and said, "I'll be with you shortly, Mrs. Reynolds. I do have some additional information to discuss with you about Claude." He returned to discussing a matter with the other doctor.

Monica took a seat in the waiting room, but it wasn't long before the doctor left and Dan came to her side. "Would you come into my spider web?" he whispered as he took her hand and led her into his office. He closed the door and immediately took her into his arms. "Did I play that cool enough, Mrs. Reynolds?" he chuckled. He proceeded to kiss her until she gently pushed him away.

"Apparently there wasn't any other information about Claude, Dr. Wilder. You gave me quite a scare when you played it so professionally. Do you think we're still in the clear after you sent the intern to give me your message in the cafeteria yesterday?"

"Oh, Sure, I gave him a good professional reason why we were meeting, and I think he bought it. However, he did have one of those rather inquisitive smiles on his face, now that I think about it. Do you think we should be quivering in our boots, Mrs. Reynolds?" We may be called to the office and get the paddle used on us. I do remember those paddles, too."

"I'm not going to worry about it, Dr. Wilder, because I have placed all that in God's hands, and He told me to let you handle it," she giggled.

"Shall we get out of this hospital then and go to the farm? I have some clothes in my car, you can change out of those nice dressy slacks, and then we'll go for a long leisurely ride on my favorite horses. How does that sound?"

"It would sound great if I didn't have to be at work at 11 o'clock tonight."

"Oh, I forgot."

"We could take a short ride, a quick dinner, and possibly a little nap before work?"

"That works for me."

Monday was a good day for Dr. Wilder because he got to release Mr. Reynolds, who promised to watch his diet a little more carefully and would definitely exercise. His son had agreed that his dad needed to do that, and he would help him set up a routine to follow before he returned to Fort Collins.

Another patient, Mrs. Wichard, was also ready to be released. She had been giving him a scolding for the last two or three days because she felt fine and just wanted to be back home. When he'd visited her room yesterday to inform her that she was getting her wish to go home, she'd remarked, "There is one thing that I'm really going to miss about my stay in this big, old hospital, though, and that is sweet little Liz Becker who has come to visit me almost daily. She could carry on a conversation about any subject that I brought up, plus a few of her own, and she was just so interested in all us old folks." She had sighed and then said with a hearty chuckle, "I wish I could take her with me."

"I guess I'll have to talk to Liz and tell her she shouldn't be spoiling all you 'old folks' who are in this hospital," he retorted in a laughing manner. "But, Mrs. Wichard, aren't you gonna miss me just an itsy bitsy bit?"

"I've missed you for years, Danny Boy, but you had better leave that sweetie alone or I'll have to come back here and take you down a notch or two. Remember, I knew you when you were still in diapers and being raised by a nanny because your parents didn't have time for you. At least that's the way it seemed. I'm sorry, I probably shouldn't have said that, but it was a shame how they ignored you when you were growing up."

"That's all right, Mrs. Wichard, my nanny was a great person, and I think I've turned out fairly well. I regret that the relationship with my parents hasn't improved much over the years, but I do have some good memories. My life is in God's hands these days, thanks to a roommate in college, and I'm happier right now than I have been in my whole life." His big smile must've really given him away.

"Oh, Danny Boy, do I detect a slight hint that there may be a creature of the opposite sex that you could be interested in?" She cocked her head and tried to flutter her eyelashes, but they just wouldn't cooperate the way she wanted. "Getting old is the pits, you know, so you need to live and love while everything still works. You do get my point, don't you?"

"I think I'd better get your release papers signed and get you out of here before you have my whole future planned for me," and as he scurried out the door, the sound of her soft laughter made him grin and just shake his head.

July was slipping by rather quickly as Monica worked the 11-7 shift for a week and then the 3-11 shift through the 26th. She and Dan had decided they'd go to Denver on her next weekend off, the 30th and 31st of July. She was working the day shift again so they could leave late afternoon on Friday and return Sunday evening. She was getting so excited because it seemed like ages since she had gotten to go out of town. Dan had suggested that they find a nice restaurant with dancing Friday night, take in a ballgame Saturday, and then visit the zoo on Sunday, if she didn't mind, along with some of the other tourist spots of Denver. She was a little surprised that he was so interested in visiting another zoo, but he had told her that he'd never been able to go to a zoo when he was growing up. They'd already gone to the zoo in Colorado Springs, on one of the days they had spent together, but since she also loved animals, it certainly didn't bother her that he wanted to visit another zoo.

When the day arrived, she could hardly wait for 3 o'clock, and Trudy and Ann had to give her a big hug and a wish for a wonderful weekend. With Dan dropping by the nurses' station fairly often, taking her to lunch, and sometimes meeting her when she got off work, there was no way they hadn't learned what was going on and were so excited for her. Trudy had been working the Sunday her father-in-law had been admitted and saw Dan holding her hand as they started toward the chapel. She had told Monica that she had also seen the big smile on her mother-in-law's face as she had walked slightly behind them.

Dan was at the farm waiting when she got home. Arrangements had been made for Charlotte and Clint to look after the horses, and Prudence, Monica's other close friend, and her husband, Derrick, were going to help out, too.

She quickly showered and dressed in some comfortable traveling shorts and top. She had packed her suitcase the night before so they were soon on their way. It was such a great July day, and luckily, a little cooler than had been predicted. It had actually dropped about 10 degrees, when some clouds blocked out the sun. "I sure hope we don't get another one of those surprise storms," Dan remarked as he'd put the top down on the convertible.

They were really enjoying the ride, but when they were about fifteen miles from the outskirts of Denver, they heard what they thought was an explosion. They looked at each other questioningly and then glanced around the area to see if they could figure out what it had been. All of a sudden, Monica yelled, "Dan, over there! I can see fire coming out of the front door of that house. Do you think anyone could be inside who needs help?"

"Take my cell phone and call 9-1-1 just in case. We'll get over there and see if there is anything we can do to help until the rescue unit arrives." Luckily there was an exit ramp, so he gave her the county road number as he turned onto the blacktop highway and then onto the narrow country road. Very shortly they were in the driveway of the house where they'd seen the flames and saw now that they were getting bigger all the time. They jumped out of the car and Dan went one way around the house while Monica went the other. When she rounded the first corner of the house, Monica heard, "Please help. Somebody, please help."

Monica glanced up to see where the cry was coming from and saw a young woman, probably close to her own age, in a second floor window holding a baby in her arms.

"Dan, around here!" she called and then she saw him come around the back corner of the house. "There's a mother and baby up there in the window," she explained and Dan was below the window immediately. Very calmly, Dan talked to the young mother, asking her what her situation was.

She explained, between sobs, that she had come up to change the baby and then she'd heard this horrible explosion that shook the whole house. "The fire filled the stairway almost immediately so I couldn't get downstairs, and it's moving awfully fast toward this room," she cried out. She was becoming hysterical, but Dan, very softly but persuasively, asked her to drop the baby and he would catch him and hand him to Monica. He had seen the blue outfit the baby was wearing and assumed that it was a boy.

He then explained that she must climb into the window and be ready to drop into his arms. He assured her than he would not let either of them hit the ground. She was hesitant, but he insisted that she must hurry because the fire was getting worse every minute. "Please, drop the baby, don't throw him, but just let him drop down to me."

She was able to follow his instructions and soon the baby and its mother were safe on the ground. Monica took the mother to the car because she was so white she was afraid she could faint any minute. She reached for the baby, when she was seated, and hugged it tightly against her. Monica's heart ached for the day she could possibly hug a baby of her own.

They heard the fire engine turn from the highway. At about the same time, they saw and heard an old tractor pulling into the back yard. A young man came running and shouting "Is my wife and baby OK? What in the world happened? He was as pale as his wife, so Dan took his arm and led him to the car to see for himself that his family was safe. They had not been injured or burned.

The firemen did what they could, but anyone could see that the house was going to be a total loss. Dan learned that Neil and Susan had just leased the house and land from a man who had wanted to give up farming and move to the city to be near his son. Everything had seemed fine then and they had lived here for about four months.

Asking a few more questions, the firemen determined that the water heater must have blown up when Susan told them she'd just turned the dishwasher on before she and the baby went upstairs. Since it uses hot water, it most likely had caused the water heater to come on and, apparently, it was getting old and had become faulty. They assured them that the fire examiner would determine the exact cause when he came to check it out. Neil and Susan appeared to be in complete shock so Dan tried to get their mind concentrating on what they had to do now. He started, of course, by asking the young couple if they had someplace they could go, and they said his parents lived about 5 miles down the road. Since the garage was not destroyed, they'd be able to go there and stay as they had before they got this chance to farm. Neil then told how they had been married almost three years when he had lost his job because of all the lay-offs in the small town where he'd been working. Susan was pregnant by then and his folks had graciously taken them in. "Now, what am I going to do?" He put his face in his hands and they could hear his uncontrollable sobs.

Dan put his hand on the young man's shoulder. "In times like these, we need to put our faith in God, Neil. We don't always understand why things happen, but if we believe in God's love for us, we can also accept the fact that things will work out for the best. I like to think of the story of Abraham, when God had asked him to sacrifice his only son to prove he had faith in Him. Abraham didn't even hesitate to obey God's command, and in the end, he was provided a lamb for the sacrifice in place of his son. May I ask what type of work you were doing before you were hit with the downsizing?"

"I was an assistant to a doctor who had his own practice in a small town just east of Denver. It was sort of like taking my residency in a hospital, but he got permission for me to do that part of my training in his clinic. He was wonderful and I learned a lot from him, but the number of patients dropped, with all the unemployment going on, so he couldn't keep me on. I don't blame him, you know, because he kept me as long as he possibly could. I couldn't find another position open, so finally decided to try farming. I don't think I'm cut out to be a farmer, but I'll do it to put food on the table for my family."

When he found out the schooling and training Neil had received, Dan asked if he'd be willing to move away from this area, if a position could be found for him.

"We'd be willing to move almost anywhere if I could find something in the medical field, but since I haven't finished my training, it's not very likely I'll have much luck."

When he heard that, Dan asked for his full name, address, and phone number where he could be reached, and then said he would be in touch with him. "It may take me a week or so, but I'll get back in touch, Neil, and I mean that." He got one of his business cards out of his pocket and handed it to him. "If I haven't called you by the 15th of next month, you call me. You can reach me at the hospital or at my apartment number. Well, at least you can leave a message and give me the dickens for not getting back to you," he chuckled.

Neil glanced at the card Dan had given him and gasped, "You're Dr. Wilder, the heart specialist, and you stopped to help my wife and baby? Wow, I don't know what to say." He looked into the car at his wife. "Honey, did you hear all this? This is Dr. Dan Wilder, the well known heart surgeon in Colorado Springs. Do you remember Dr. Brady mentioning his work and how he admired his talents? Oh, man, do things like this really happen?" Neil couldn't help but take Dan's hand and they did a real man's handshake.

Monica looked at Dan and saw a slight blush on his cheeks. She was pretty proud of this friend of hers, too. "Do you think we'd better be on our way, Dan? We do have a few miles left before we reach our destination." She then turned to Susan, who had gotten out of the car and stood with Neil's arm around her. "I hope we may be able to see each other again soon." Giving her a hug and a little pat on the baby's cheek, she wished her the best of luck.

As Neil and Susan stood beside the car, Dan and Monica backed out of the drive and continued their trip into Denver. What a beginning to a getaway weekend!

CHAPTER THIRTEEN

The hotel rooms were beautiful. The walls were painted a very pretty ivory but with a hint of pale green and furnished with French Provincial furniture. Comforters and drapes in shades of green and brown added color in the bedrooms, and there was a dark brown leather chair close to the window with a table and lamp near by. Dan had reserved a two-bedroom suite and from the sitting room windows you could see a small park that looked inviting with the shade from the tall stately trees. The lush bushes and flowers were perfectly manicured and the colors were still brilliant for late July. The benches scattered here and there were in use by sightseers or weary walkers, and it made for a great relaxing view. The sitting room was very comfortable with a large damask couch, two very comfortable recliners and nice lamps on the two end tables. A coffee table completed that area, and a small kitchenette was along the opposite wall.

Dan had taken charge of having their luggage put in the right rooms, and then he'd come to sit beside her. "It certainly feels good to relax, after our little rescue job earlier, but I'm starting to get awfully thirsty. I guess I should've gotten something for us before I sat down. There are sodas, wine, crackers, cheese and dip. What's your pleasure?" he asked as he started to get back up.

"Stay seated, Dan, and let me check it out." She was up and heading for the small refrigerator in the kitchenette, but Dan was right beside her.

"We'll check it out together then, because I am not going to be waited on by you this weekend." When they reached the refrigerator, Dan stepped in front of the door and took her in his arms. "This is what I really need," he said as his lips met hers and she found herself reacting eagerly.

What am I letting myself in for? she wondered as her arms went around his neck and she was sure she was in over her head. To her surprise, Dan stopped the kiss, stepped back, and gave her that grin which could've clinched her throwing away the key to her heart.

"I guess it's a good thing we have our separate bedrooms, Sweetheart, because those kisses of yours make me think of everything but being a good boy tonight." He turned then and opened the refrigerator door to see what the hotel had supplied for them. They settled for some cheese and sodas, plus some snack crackers that were on the counter. "We'll eat just enough to hold us until we can clean up and get to the restaurant," Dan remarked. "I'm really looking forward to dancing with you again. It seems like such a long time since we went dancing after that big storm."

"Hopefully I can keep my eyes open long enough to eat and dance," she grinned as she let out a big yawn. She took a bite of the cheese and crackers she'd put together. They both were rather quiet as they enjoyed the snacks and watched the news on TV.

An hour or so later, Dan awoke and found Monica curled up asleep beside him. She looked so comfortable and relaxed, he hated to wake her, but they would be late for their reservation at the restaurant if they didn't start getting cleaned up. "Mauni," he whispered as he ran his fingers down her cheek, "we've got to get moving."

She sat up quickly and yawned, "I can't believe I fell asleep. Why did you let me sleep so long?" she exclaimed as she glanced at her watch.

"Because, I just awoke myself. We've got to get cleaned up now or we'll be late for our reservation at the restaurant. Are you all right?"

"Oh, yes, I'm fine now that I had my little nap." She was up quickly and on her way to get changed for the first big night of their weekend together.

The dress she'd brought for tonight was a very simple peach silk which was sleeveless and styled with a modestly low Vee neckline, a snug fitting bodice and a slightly gathered skirt flaring to a handkerchief hem which was fluttery as it reached her calves. White sandals with 3" heels and white dangling earrings completed the outstanding ensemble. Dan, dressed in a light tan summer suit, white shirt and a light tan figured tie, could only do a weak whistle when she came out of her bedroom. "You're the picture of absolute splendor, Mauni," and he was on his way to kiss her on the cheek.

The restaurant was simply gorgeous, and Monica wondered how Dan had known to make the reservations here. When they'd been seated in a secluded booth with a curved seat just made for two, she looked to see if she could read anything in his expression. She could see nothing except a satisfied smile, so she asked, "Dan, how do you know so much about Denver when you told me you didn't go anywhere after you started working?"

Turning toward her, he took her hand and kissed the palm, ran his fingers up her arm onto her neck and then tilting her chin, he kissed her gently but lovingly. "The word, 'after' is the key there, Mauni. Before I started practicing, I was an intern and also did my residency here in Denver. Six, and sometimes eight, of us would regularly check out the big city once or twice a month. There were both guys and gals so we'd sometimes act like we were on a date, if there were the right number of each, and we'd hit the restaurants, nightclubs, and even some hotels where we knew there would be music and a dance floor.

My dad, at that time, was still paying my bills, so I took advantage, to a degree. I didn't really try to punish him for ignoring me while I was growing up, but I felt like I needed a little recreation and fun during those hectic days, too. I must've been conservative enough, because I knew he would put his foot down if I went too far."

"I see that there's a lot I still need to learn about you, Dr. Wilder, and I have a sneaky suspicion that you aren't going to be too forthcoming with it. I guess I'll just have to find a way to open your secret vault of information."

The server arrived at that time with a plate of appetizers and two glasses of wine, and Monica again looked at him suspiciously. "Did you select the whole dinner when you made the reservation?" she asked, but she only got that tantalizing smile as her answer. Well, she was hungry, so whatever he'd ordered, she was sure she would enjoy it. Her first bite of the stuffed mushroom was so delicious she couldn't help kissing his cheek. She also was having fun nibbling on the relishes that had surrounded the mushrooms, until their entree arrived. She was thrilled to see a filet mignon, small red parsley potatoes and a wonderful fresh side salad. When they'd finished that course, she was thinking that he surely hadn't ordered a big dessert, too.

He took her hand and pulled her onto the dance floor. "We'll have to work some of that dinner off before we can eat our dessert," he said as he twirled her out of his arms. It was a rather fast song and she was hoping the next one would be slow because her stomach was reacting to all that swing and sway. She lucked out, and it was so exciting to be held so close to him and to dance cheek to cheek. *He must be at least 3 inches taller than Terry was.*

After two more slow dances and then a fast one, he led her back to their booth. The server appeared and asked if they were ready to have their dessert served. Dan nodded and within minutes the chef arrived to fix a Cherry Jubilee at their table. Monica was impressed, and she could do nothing but stare. "I'll have to learn how to do that," she whispered.

"I think that is something we should leave to the experts and just enjoy the fruits of their labor," he chuckled as he pulled her into his arms and kissed her forehead.

When they'd finished their dessert and danced a few more dances, they realized they were exhausted and should head for the hotel. Monica could only imagine that she was still living in a fairytale world.

When they reached their suite, Dan surprised her by saying, "Sweetheart, you could probably sleep beside me tonight and I would never know you were there. I'm so tired I'll be asleep as soon as I hit the pillow." He gave her a sweet gentle goodnight kiss and headed her toward her room. "I'll never believe I said that when I wake up in the morning, but right now I've got to say, Goodnight Sweetheart, I'm sure I'll see you in my dreams."

Monica fell on her knees beside her bed and prayed, "I still have no idea, Dear Jesus, why you have been so good to me. I was ready to live alone the rest of my life when Terry was lost in Iraq, but here I am having the time of my life with Dan, a man who is so far above most gentlemen. I have to thank you for giving me this chance. I was apprehensive, as you know, about this weekend, but my fears have vanished and I'm going to put my future in your hands. Please give Dan and me a good night's rest and a weekend to remember for a lifetime. Thank you again, Lord, for your patience and love toward all your children. Amen."

She had hardly gotten her gown on and climbed onto the big comfortable bed before she was sound asleep. She hoped she wasn't a sleepwalker because her thoughts, and most likely her dreams, would be taking her across the sitting room and into his bed to snuggle up against those muscles she had felt while they'd been dancing.

Dan awoke and reached for the beautiful woman he'd been holding in his dreams. He was disappointed that she was not there in person, but relieved that he'd had the sense to treat her like the Lord would have wanted him to. He got out of bed, showered and dressed, and then went to the kitchen to make some coffee. Apparently, Monica was still sleeping, but he was surprised to see that her door was ajar. He had expected it to be locked. He wanted to look in to see her, but resisted the urge and started the coffee instead.

After he got the coffee brewing, however, he just had to peek, and when he saw her lying there so content, he found himself by her bed stroking her arm and brushing her hair back from her face. She opened her eyes dreamily and smiled up at him. "Did you sleep as well as I did?" she purred. "I don't think I moved a muscle all night. Maybe you'd like to curl up beside me for a few minutes."

"Monica Reynolds, I think you, of all people, should know what those actions could lead to," but as he stood there watching her, he realized she wasn't fully awake.

Suddenly it registered in her mind that she was no longer dreaming and that the real Dr. Dan Wilder was standing right beside her bed. She sat up quickly, pulling the sheet up to her neck. "Dan, what are you doing in my room?" Her face was hot as she wondered what she'd said that would've caused him to make a remark like that.

Dan chuckled then as he realized she'd definitely been half asleep, but he hoped he'd been the one she was asking to curl up with her. "I just came in to see if you were going to join me sometime today or continue in your dream world. I'm afraid my hormones wouldn't behave this morning if I were to curl up beside you on the bed, as you so sweetly invited. So, come on, Sleepy Head, the coffee is ready and I'm getting hungry. I'll call room service while you take your shower and get dressed." He turned and quickly left the room.

Monica was so embarrassed as she tried to remember what she had said, but when she glanced at her watch, she nearly fainted. "How could I have slept until 9 o'clock?" She went to hurriedly shower and dress in white crop pants and an aqua v-neck tee for the game they'd be going to this afternoon. She'd noticed that Dan was also dressed very casually in his khaki shorts and a white polo shirt. *Just how many more surprises are there in store for me this weekend?* she sighed as she still concentrated on when this fairytale would end.

They leisurely ate their breakfast in the suite, strolled over to the park they had seen from the sitting room windows, and decided to follow a trail they discovered leading into a wooded area. It turned out to be a nature trail, and they really enjoyed seeing the different birds and hearing their songs, and also the other small animals that scurried around in the foliage and trees. They came to a small rippling stream where they spotted a doe with her fawn taking advantage of the cool water and the green stretch of grass.

When they got back from their hike, they decided they'd just stop for a light salad on their way to the Mile-high Stadium because they certainly wanted to enjoy a hot dog with all the trimmings at the game. They'd arrived a little early, but it was fun watching the players as they signed autographs for the kids and the other pre-game activities.

The game started right at 2 o'clock. It was exciting and close. There wasn't a single hit or run during the first four innings, but then a solo home run apparently sparked the home team. They went on to win 6 to 3, which made most of the fans happy.

After leaving the game, Dan drove around for quite a while showing her the hospital, the apartment complex where he had lived, and some of the hang-outs he and the others had frequented. They had planned to stop for pizza on the way back to the hotel, but neither of them were that hungry so they opted for an ice cream cone. Again they were exhausted and ready to relax on the sofa in each other's arms. After a few wonderful kisses, a discussion of sorts about the day, and watching some news on TV, they headed to their separate rooms.

Sunday morning Monica again slept later than usual and decided it had to be the bed. She vowed she was going to buy a new mattress as soon as she could afford one. "But for now, I'd better shower and get dressed," she mumbled, "before Dan has to come and pull me out of the most heavenly resting place."

"Did you say something, Mrs. Reynolds? I'm glad to hear that you've finally decided to wake up. Could I bring you a cup of coffee?" She could see him standing just outside her door in the little kitchenette.

"No, Dan, I was just talking to myself, but I'll get dressed and then have my coffee out there, if that's all right with you."

"That's fine. Just don't linger too long if we're going to get to church on time."

Dan had mentioned there was a church just a block from the hotel, so they were going to attend the services and then go to the zoo, museum, and other sights around Denver before starting home around 5 o'clock. She decided the sundress she had packed, which had lots of tiny flowers on a white background and the full skirt falling just to her knees, would be quite appropriate for the day's activities. She would wear the high-heeled sandals to church and then change to her walking sandals for the rest of the day.

She found Dan relaxing in one of the comfortable recliners in the sitting room with a cup of coffee and the Sunday paper, compliments of the hotel. He looked so handsome in his bone-colored slacks and navy polo shirt that she must've swooned audibly. Looking up from the paper, he whistled and gave her a slow top to bottom survey. "Aren't you the lovely one this morning? Shall I order breakfast brought up, or would you like to eat down in the hotel restaurant for a change today?"

"I'd like to enjoy another breakfast right here in our room, Dan. It's so romantic with just the two of us."

"Are you really looking for romance, Mauni? I'd really love to satisfy your needs."

"Dan, behave yourself. Do you know what you're going to order?"

"Of course, but what do you want?" He was chuckling as he patted the little bit of space in the chair beside him. "Come here and sit beside me while I call for room service, and then we'll have a little romance before our food is delivered. Would that start your day off on a high note?"

He smiled so devilishly she was tempted to go to the phone and just order for herself.

"Maybe I won't eat with you this morning if you're going to act that way," and she put a little pout on her lips.

"Ah, come on, My Little Sweetheart, give me a smile, an order for breakfast, and a good morning kiss before I get out of this chair and smother you with so many kisses you'll beg me to take you to bed."

"Well, if you put it that way," she smiled. "I'll have the 'Eye Opener' and here's your morning kiss." She put her finger to her mouth and then touched his cheek, but not quickly enough to prevent his arm from reaching around and pulling her onto his lap.

He successfully captured her lips with his for a great beginning to the day, and then he called room service to place their order.

After another wonderful breakfast in their suite, Dan had the luggage put in the car, while he checked out, and they were on their way for another exciting day. The church was a large stone building with beautiful stained glass windows, padded pews, and carpeted floors. The organ was playing softly as they entered, which gave such a reverence to the sanctuary. The narthex had been quite busy and noisy with people visiting, but they were soon entering silently for the beginning of the service.

CHAPTER FOURTEEN

After an inspiring church service, they had gone to the zoo and were almost through the museum when Monica felt the pain that she had been introduced to a few months before Terry had to leave for Iraq. *Please, not now,* she whispered to herself, as she remembered her gynecologist encouraging her and Terry to have a child before it was too late for her to conceive. They had tried, until Terry had gone off to war, with the hope that he would come home to an addition to their family.

Of course, it hadn't happened and now she is a widow. She didn't know how long she had before she would need to have a hysterectomy that would end all her hopes of having the baby she had wanted for years. The doctor had said then that it was her first attack and from all the exams she had done, it appeared Monica might have four to six years. Endometriosis is unpredictable, however, and an exact timetable was impossible to judge.

Monica had become quiet all of a sudden, and when Dan glanced at her and saw the signs of pain in her eyes and on her face, he stopped abruptly. "Mauni, what's the matter? I know you're hurting for some reason, so don't tell me it's nothing."

"I think it must be about time for my period," she lied, "but I'll be OK. Let's finish the museum and then, if you don't mind, I'd like to start home."

"The museum can wait. If you're not feeling well, we are heading home right now." He took her by the arm and started toward the door of the museum and on to the car.

"I don't want to spoil your day, Dan," she pleaded as he opened the car door and helped her inside. "I'm sure I could finish the tour."

"Hush," he said as he shut the door and went around to get in his side. He left the top up so they could have a little air conditioning and not all the wind blowing through her hair.

"Do you normally have this much pain with your periods, or is it something different this month? I haven't noticed you showing any signs of being uncomfortable before, but I guess we haven't known each other for very long, either. Is this your first period since we met? Please be honest with me, Mauni. I want to know exactly how you feel and if this is some-thing other than normal for you. Should I take you to the emergency room?"

"Dan, please don't embarrass me by making me talk about personal matters. I'll get an appointment this week and prove to you that I'm in fine shape."

He dropped the subject and headed toward home. It wasn't long until he glanced over to see the charred remains of the house where they had met Neil and Susan. "I wonder how they're doing," Dan remarked, but Monica could tell from the tone of his voice that his mind wasn't really on Neil and Susan at that moment. He'd been watching her almost constantly.

"What can I say to make you stop worrying about me?" she asked, but nothing came to her and he had just shrugged. She tried to get comfortable and enjoy the ride home. When a pain would occasionally hit, she'd quickly turn her face toward the window to prevent Dan from seeing her grimace.

When they finally reached the farm, they saw the horses and riders coming toward the barn. Monica thought it would be Charlotte and Clint, but it turned out to be Prudence and Derrick. Dan was retrieving their suitcases from the trunk and Monica hadn't quite reached the back door of the house when a van pulled into the drive and Charlotte and Clint hopped out. "You're early," Charlotte called, but as she got closer, she saw the look on her friend's face that she had seen only twice before. The first was when she had discovered she suffered from endometriosis, and the other was when she'd learned that Terry had been killed. *What is causing it this time?* She wondered if the weekend hadn't gone well or if it's her health.

"I have something to talk to you about, Monica. Could we go into the house and have a private time, please?" Turning toward Clint and Dan, she called, "Hey, guys, would you go help Derrick with the horses and send Prudence to the house? I'd sure appreciate it."

Dan didn't know what to think about the situation, but when Charlotte's look assured him that she would take care of Monica, he turned and went with Clint to the barn. When Clint told Prudence that Charlotte had asked them to send her to the house, she took off on a run as if she knew it was serious. Dan was beside himself, only wanting to barge into that house and demand some answers, but he knew he couldn't do that. He'd have to wait until someone was ready to tell him what was going on with Monica. It wasn't easy for him to do because she had become a major part of his life, and something was seriously wrong.

About a half-hour later, Charlotte and Prudence came outside and said they'd gotten Monica to lie down and rest. Charlotte took Dan's hand and pulled him over to a spot where they could have a quiet conversation. "Dan, I know you're concerned about her as we all are, but I'm not going to break my promise to her by telling you what is going on. She has to do that or nothing will be right between you. I'll just say that she's not in any immediate danger, and she'll see her gynecologist this week to find out what her future holds. I've probably said too much already, since you're a doctor, but I just hope you'll be there for her."

"Thanks, Charlotte, and don't worry, I'll be there for her, whatever the problem. But, right now, should I stick around or would she feel better if I were gone?"

"I hope you'll stay for a while and be here when she wakes up. We wouldn't want her to think that you turn tail and run when a little problem arises, now, would we?" She had a most convincing smile, and Dan felt much better knowing that Monica's friends had confided in him and were not blaming him for her discomfort. He could, however, read between the lines enough to grasp the possibility that Monica might have a serious female problem and will need to have surgery. It could also mean she may not be able to have children which he knew would be devastating to her from some of their conversations. Of course, since there's more than one possibility, he'll have to discover the real problem and then see what they can do about finding a solution for it.

The two couples had left for a meeting at the church so he was alone with his own thoughts while Monica slept. Finally, she came into the kitchen about 8 o'clock and was a little surprised and embarrassed that he was still there. She was feeling much better but had awakened hungry since they hadn't stopped to eat coming home. He'd checked the pantry and refrigerator, but there wasn't much that could be fixed quickly, so he offered to go and get something at the nearest fast food restaurant.

"I feel up to riding with you," she giggled as her stomach growled to let them know they'd better hurry. They drove to the highway and found a place where they could get a big sandwich and fries. She didn't say anything more about her problem, so he decided to let her have her little secret for the time being.

"Are you going to try to work tomorrow?" he asked as he prepared to leave a little while later. "Maybe you should take a day off and just rest. I'm sorry, Monica, if I pushed you too hard this weekend. We did do a lot of things in a short time."

"I don't need to take a day off, Dan, and please, don't think it's your fault. Just let me see the doctor this week and find out what is going on, and then I promise I'll give you all the details, as much as I hate to talk about it."

"Monica Reynolds, will you please remember that I'm a doctor and I have confronted all kinds of problems during the last five or six years? I'll understand when you're ready to tell me. I just hope you can trust me enough to let me share your concern and maybe help to find a solution. I'll go now so you can get a good night's rest. Thanks for a great weekend."

Monica saw her gynecologist, Lucille Moore, Tuesday afternoon after her shift was over at the hospital. The diagnosis was that this flare-up means the time for getting pregnant is growing shorter. Lucille estimated that she might still have between three and four years, and that would be long enough to maybe have two babies, but then the surgery would most likely be imminent. "Are you dating anyone that might have some husband potential?" she asked. "I've heard something about you and that big handsome Dr. Wilder seeing each other. Is there any truth in the rumors?"

"Gossip certainly travels fast, doesn't it?" she giggled. She was blushing noticeably but confessed that they had been seeing each other, but she couldn't be sure if he had any thoughts of marriage in his head. "He is the most wonderful guy, so attentive, so much fun to be with, so handsome---but marriage, I have no idea."

"Well, if you would like to have a relationship with him, maybe you'll just have to be a little more direct about your problem and wishes."

"That's much easier said than done, Lucille, but maybe I can figure out something that will work. Thanks for your time, suggestions, and concern for me. I'll keep you posted as my time flies by." She left the office in a dejected mood thinking there was only a slight chance she would ever be able to become a mother, but could she even suggest to Dan the plan she was forming in her mind? She doubted it.

CHAPTER FIFTEEN

Monday and Tuesday had been hectic for Dan as he had been in OR all morning both days. His appointment calendar had been full in the afternoons, and he'd also been called for an emergency Monday evening because of a car accident with several injured. He hadn't had a chance to even speak to Monica on Monday, and he'd been afraid, for awhile, that Tuesday was going to be exactly the same.

He was glad when he was able to be home by 8:30. He dropped into his favorite old recliner, picked up his cell, and dialed her number. When there was no answer, he was upset, disappointed and worried. "Where is she?" he asked himself as his mind went all directions. He'd left a message so maybe, if she was at the barn, she would call back when she got to the house. He tried to read the paper, watch TV, and look at his schedule for tomorrow, but none of them interested him. He wanted to talk to Monica.

It was almost 10 o'clock and he still hadn't heard from her. He was getting his shoes back on, so he could drive out there, when the phone rang. "Dan, it's Monica," she said when he answered. He didn't know whether to scream at her, cry because he had been so scared or just thank God that she was all right. "Dan?" she then asked, "are you all right? I'd decided to go for a ride tonight because I thought I could think more clearly in the cool night air, but I'm still confused and without an answer. You've had two very busy days, haven't you? I saw the OR schedule and it looked like your name was there constantly. Are you taking it easy now? I see from your call that you were home by 8:30." She hesitated then and waited for him to say something, but there was only silence. "Dan," she tried again, "what did you call me for? If you don't want to talk, I'll let you go."

"Don't hang up, Monica. I was listening to your voice and wishing you were here. "

"It has seemed a little lonely without you around to pester me," she giggled.

"Well, I'd been realizing how much I miss you, but not to pester you. To have such a wonderful weekend, and then nothing for two whole days, it was like the wind going out of a balloon. Have you been busy on 4th floor, too?"

"It's been a rat race with hardly a chance to get a drink of water, let alone get a lunch break. We certainly could have used a couple more nurses. Is tomorrow going to be another heavy one?"

"Not according to my schedule, and I'm planning to take the afternoon off. I was just wondering if I could come out and see you when you get home. I just want to see that you're OK, and if you've had the appointment with Dr. Moore, will you be ready to tell me about it. I won't push for details, Mauni, but I do care about you and want to help, if possible."

"Do you really want to help me, Dan? I've been thinking about something, but I'm hesitant to bring it up because it's not what I would normally even consider."

"Why don't you hold that thought so we can discuss it face to face? I'll be there when you get home tomorrow. Will that be OK?"

"Yes, that will be fine. I'll be looking forward to seeing you tomorrow. I'd better say goodnight now because I have some things to do around here before I go to bed."

"Goodnight, Sweetheart." Dan leaned back into his chair and released a sigh as if he had been holding his breath. *What has she been thinking about that she normally wouldn't even consider? I hope tonight and tomorrow go really fast or I'm going to be one big basket case.* He grinned as several thoughts were racing through his head.

❧

Three o'clock finally arrived and Monica headed home, so anxious to see Dan, but so undecided about presenting her plan to him. She could only wonder whether he would be willing to help her, or just stare at her like she was crazy. She figured she'd just have to play it by ear and see how things went. She was pretty sure he really cared for her, but would he go this far to help her?

Dan was sitting in the sun porch when she turned into the drive, but he was quickly at the car, opening the door for her, and taking her into his arms. "I've missed you so much, and you must know how much I need a kiss." He lifted her up and held her against him as his lips played havoc with her senses.

If she could play her cards right, her plan would be easy to pull off right now, but she shouldn't trick him into something. She wanted him to consent fully to doing what she had in mind. "You'd better put me down before you hurt your back," she smiled as she looked into those beautiful blue eyes.

"Put you down, never! I'm going to keep you tight in my arms until you tell me how much you've missed me."

"Well, let me see. I had to show the horses how much I missed them over the long weekend, and I had to tell Trudy and Ann how much I missed them while I was gone, and I had to tell the patients, who were still there, how much I had missed them, and then I had to call Char and Pru and tell them thanks and how much I missed them, and...."

He let her down slowly until her feet touched the ground and then let out a sigh. "I can see about what place I hold in your list of loves, so I guess I'll just take off and go home." He didn't know for sure whether to be truly disappointed or to be happy that she could still tease him, but he turned to walk toward his car.

She quickly grabbed his arm and turned him back around. "You're not getting away that easily, Doc. I have some work that I need a big strong handsome man for, and your pay will be supper and a really long talk with me. I've missed you terribly the last two days, and I want to spend some special quality time with you. Are you ready to let me?"

"Well, now, that sounds intriguing. Are you going to give me a hint as to what it is, or are you going to make me wait until I'm weak with anticipation?"

"Oh, I don't want you to be weak. I need a strong, handsome, ready-to-go man to carry out my plan. Come on in the house, Superman, and I'll see if you fit my requirements." She was laughing as she grabbed his hand and pulled him toward the house.

What has she got up her sleeve? he wondered as he followed obediently up the steps to the sun porch, through the kitchen into the living room, and then into the hall leading to the bedrooms and bath. She turned into her own bedroom.

She turned to look at him, from his hair down to his shoes. In his denim shorts and a nice bright yellow polo shirt, he really did look like her superman. But she was building up to the fulfillment of her plan, so she cuddled up quite close to him and then tugged at his shirt until she got it out of his shorts. She then proceeded to pull it over his head.

He *was* staring at her, but there was a twinkle in his eyes, too. "Mauni, you'd better be sure what you're doing here in your bedroom. I could easily get carried away."

"Could you? It's going to be too hot to work in these." She could only whisper now as she concentrated on undoing the button on his shorts. That's when he took her hands and stopped the action. Of course, he'd noticed that they were trembling and her face had turned a rosy red.

"Sorry, Sweetheart, but something is not going quite right here. You are shaking and definitely not my 'in control' Mauni. Do you want to tell me about it? I think I've pretty well guessed what you're facing, and this is definitely not the solution you're looking for."

Monica burst into tears, and he pulled her into his arms. "Sweetheart, let's go in the living room and talk about this. He picked up his shirt and pulled it back over his head. He then took her hand and led her to the couch. He held her until the sobbing stopped, and then he looked at her and smiled. "I'm flattered, Monica Reynolds, that you would want me in that capacity, but there is a much better way."

"You mean you would help me get pregnant without me having to practically force you to go to bed with me? Oh, Dan, I was so humiliated and naive while I was doing that to you, but I'm getting desperate. My gynecologist told me yesterday that the endometriosis is getting worse, and if I don't get pregnant soon, I may never be able to have a baby. When I was first diagnosed over two years ago, she suggested that Terry and I try to have a child as soon as possible, but you know he went to Iraq and we weren't successful before he left. I was told then I might have five or six years left, but now it's down to three or four. I can't imagine living the rest of my life without ever having a baby to hold in my arms. So, I was wondering if you would consider helping me get pregnant. I wouldn't ask for anything, Dan, and you wouldn't have to be obligated at all as far as the baby is concerned."

"Honey, you are really something else, you know that? Are you telling me that you would not *want* me to be obligated after I got you pregnant? I get a night or two of bliss, or however long it takes, and then I could just walk away? I really don't know what to say. It sounds way too good to be true, and you've heard that old saying, haven't you? If it sounds too good to be true, it probably is. To me, that is because I couldn't live with myself if I did something like that, and besides, what would God think of me?

Now, let me give you my plan, my sweet adorable Monica Reynolds. I'd absolutely love trying to give you as many babies as we can fit into the time you have left, before you have to have the surgery, but only on one condition. That condition, Sweetheart, is that I am your husband and you are my wife. Now, what would you say to that proposal?"

"I couldn't ask you to do that, Dan. You have been wonderful and attentive and we've had such great fun, but I know all about you not wanting to get serious with any girl, and you have your apartment where you hide out. You've called me all those sweet names, and I've felt so very special, but I've tried so hard not to take them seriously because I thought you'd be walking away any day. I felt like Cinderella at the ball, but I didn't know when 12 o'clock would be striking and you'd be gone. So, when I got the report yesterday and knew the time was getting short, I thought if I could only get you to help me get pregnant, I could have the baby and no one else would have to be involved."

"You're right, Sweetie, when you say that I've been

attentive, and I've definitely tried to show you a good time. I've also called you all those sweet names, and every bit of it was true because I'm so in love with you. From the first time I saw you in Josh's room, I knew that I wanted to marry you. I may have acted a bit uncommitted because I knew I couldn't ask you to marry me when I pulled into your drive that same day we met." Smiling, he reached over and tilted her chin, looked into her eyes for just a moment before kissing her so very convincingly that she put her arms around his waist and hugged as hard as she could. He finally had to holler, "Please, Monica, Stop! You're stronger than you realize."

Turning to face her, he continued, "Now listen, Miss Cinderella, there's a proposal on the table, and we need to get it settled so we can get something to eat and start making plans for a wedding. Will you help me out here?"

"We've only known each other for one month and four days, Dan. What are people going to think?"

"Are you more concerned about what people are going to think or about getting that baby you want so desperately? We aren't going to get married tomorrow, but a lot of couples do get married after knowing each other for only a short time. We don't want to wait too long, though, because we want to get busy starting our family, and there are a few plans that will need to be made. So,

Sweetie, are you with me in this? Just say yes and I'll get you a ring first thing tomorrow."

He was chuckling when he continued, "You probably won't believe it, but I came so very close to buying a ring and taking it with me on the trip, just in case I had a chance to ask you to be my wife, but I didn't think you were quite ready for that step. If I had asked, would you have turned me down or would you have accepted my proposal?"

"I would've wanted to, but I probably would have been as hesitant as I am now. Oh, Dan, I have dreamed about this happening since the night of the storm when I slept in your arms on the bed of straw in the barn. I couldn't believe it would happen then, and I'm still in a daze that it is really happening now. How can I be hearing such precious words from the most elusive Dr. Dan Wilder?"

"Are you giving me the answer I want to hear in a very roundabout way, Mauni? I really wasn't being elusive; I just hadn't found the one God had picked out for me yet. Now that I've found you, won't you please just say yes and make me the happiest guy in the world tonight?"

"Oh Yes, Dan, Yes, Yes, Yes!" Her arms went around his neck and she gave him the kiss she had wanted to give him for weeks; a commitment of love from her heart that would last for as long as she had breath to breathe.

CHAPTER SIXTEEN

Monica had put a pork roast with small red potatoes, carrots and onions in the slow cooker to cook throughout the day, and the aroma was beginning to circulate all through the house to fully arouse their appetites. She'd checked the time and decided they could easily feed the horses before they ate, so they went to the barn, filled the feed troughs and cleaned the stalls. They sat on the straw bed while they talked to both of the horses about their plans, and were rather surprised when they got what they took as a whinnied approval.

Since Monica had also fixed a Jello salad that morning, everything was ready to eat when they returned to the house. She put Dan to work setting the table while she was fixing the gravy, the drinks, and dishing up the food. "I don't know how you do all this, Mauni, and still have the time or strength to work."

"It's really not too hard with all the modern appliances.

I remember, when I was little, Mom didn't have some of the things I have because we were so short on funds, but she would still have friends over and fix a great meal. I loved helping her by setting the table, and some times she'd let me cut some of the vegetables if we were having stew or homemade soup."

"Well, her teachings rubbed off on you in great style. I'm looking forward to when I can enjoy your cooking a lot. But, I was thinking that there's something else we'll have to discuss and make a decision on, Sweetie. If we're going to be concentrating on getting you with child, wouldn't it be better if you weren't working?"

"Oh, Dan, I just got started working in my nursing career. I hate to leave so soon, especially when they are so short of nurses."

"If you had to choose between the two, your nursing career or having a baby, which would you be picking?"

"That's not a fair question, Dr. Wilder. Why is it always the woman who has to give up things in order to have a baby? I think God made a mistake there, but I guess it was Eve who really gave us women the pain of childbirth. But we get the greatest pleasure, too, when we do the biggest share of caring for the baby and also the daddy," she grinned.

"Let's talk to your doctor and see what she would recommend. Of course, you can continue working until we get married, if you'd like, and the hospital can be recruiting more nurses during that time. I'll talk to them about that. So, have you given any thought to when and where you would like to tie this knot?" he chuckled.

"Gee, it's been all of four hours since you proposed, so I certainly should have all the details worked out by now, shouldn't I? Actually, all kinds of thoughts have been flashing through my head---like attendants, the church, flowers, the ceremony, and so on, but I hadn't given a thought about when. Sort of silly, I guess, because I should have a date before I start all the other preparations. I suppose you have a date all picked out, Dr. Wilder."

"Well, I've been giving it some thought, even if you haven't," he said as his lower lip extended out to playfully form a pout. "What would you think about working until the end of August and then getting married on Friday, the 2nd of September? I have always wanted to elope, and still do, actually. It sounds so exciting and daring, and since you've already been through this once, maybe you'd agree? I'll go along with anything but a big formal affair."

"No, Dan, I don't want a formal wedding, but I would prefer getting married in the church. It just seems, to me anyway, much more like God is blessing the marriage if it's held in the church. Would that be all right with you?"

"Of course, anything to please my soon-to-be wife, but can you plan a small wedding and work, too? I can hardly believe this is happening, after all the years I've spent alone."

"I think I can recruit enough help to get a small wedding planned by September 2nd, Dan, and I really like the date because I love September weather. We'll see about the church and go from there."

"Mauni, do you suppose I'm too set in my ways? Some of those cases I've read about can make a person a little hesitant."

She couldn't keep from laughing. "From what I've seen of you and your actions, I'd say that you are the least 'set in your ways' of anyone I know. If we, like most couples, have some small differences, we'll just work them out."

Dan had finally switched from a pager to a cell phone, and of course, it had to start ringing. When he finished the call, he said he had to go and apologized for not being able to help clean up the kitchen. "I'll see you tomorrow when you get off work. Why don't you bring a dressy change of clothes so we can go out to eat someplace nice? Would you like to come to my apartment to get cleaned up?"

"That sounds like a good plan." With a quick kiss goodnight, he ran to his car and was on his way to the hospital.

On his lunch hour the next day, Dan hurried to the nearby Jewelry Store. One of the doctors had recommended it, but promised to stay mum, and the clerk was very helpful with his selection. He wanted a good-sized diamond, but he didn't want it standing so tall it would interfere with her work in the barn or yard. He found exactly what he wanted, including the wedding band, and was whistling a merry tune walking back to the hospital.

He had used his cell phone earlier to make a reservation at one of the more exclusive restaurants in town where his friend, Nick, just happens to be the maitre'd. He couldn't keep the smile off his face as they'd worked on the plans for a fabulous evening. Nick had come up with some great ideas, and now Dan had some details to get done. It was a good thing his schedule was light today because all he could think of was Monica and the evening ahead for the two of them. *I'm going to give Monica an engagement ring, and she's going to be my wife,* he kept repeating over and over to himself. "Whoopee!" he shouted. He looked around sheepishly to see how many people might be staring at him, but luckily, the coast was clear.

He'd only had four fairly easy appointments and then was through for the day. He put his plan into action by going to the gift shop in the hospital. He then called Nick and they finalized their plans. Nick had been a close college friend all those years ago, but they'd lost track of each other, as it so often happens, when they'd left college. About eighteen months ago, they had renewed their acquaintance when Nick had to have emergency surgery and was at the mercy of Dan's skillful expertise. Since then, he'd been occasionally dropping in at the hospital to see Dan, always reminding him that he owed him big time. Well, tonight he was going to get a chance to repay him, and Dan knew he could trust Nick to do everything just right. With all the plans complete, he headed home and arrived only about fifteen minutes before Monica was at the door.

Their reservation wasn't until 7 o'clock so they fixed some snacks---crackers, cheese, dip, and olives---and was going to relax on the deck, but it proved to be a little too warm so they retreated to the air-conditioned living room. He *had* remembered to put some tea bags in the jug this morning for making sun tea and had set it out to do its magic. They were just sitting and enjoying the cool drink and snacks, but both were a little more quiet than usual. Dan was so afraid, if he opened his mouth, he would give away his surprise, but he'd finally put his arm across her shoulders and pulled her to him. "You're rather quiet, Mauni. Did you have a rough day or is something else bothering you?"

"Don't you go being so nonchalant, Dr. Wilder. You

remember perfectly well what happened last night and that we have a lot of plans to make. You also have me on pins and needles by asking me to bring a dressy change of clothes. I'm just wondering exactly what it is that you're going to spring on me tonight."

"Me? Spring something on you? Why, Mauni, I just wanted to take you to a nice restaurant and thought you might like to dress up a little more than usual. I thought I'd take you to Anwan's."

"You're taking me to Anwan's? Dan, that is one of the most expensive restaurants in the city. How were you able to even get a reservation? I thought they were booked for over a month in advance."

"Just lucky I guess. By the way, were you able to get another appointment with your gynecologist or did you even have time to make contact with her today?" He was so afraid he was going to give himself away, because he was so excited, but he was really surprised his voice sounded rather calm.

"I did call her on my lunch hour and she'll be able to see me, or us, tomorrow after 4 o'clock. I wasn't sure if you wanted to talk to her, too, or whether you just wanted me to find out her opinion."

"I'd love to go if it won't bother you having me tag along. Did you tell her the reason you wanted to see her again so soon?"

"Yes, and I think she's as excited as we are. Did I mention that she'd heard the rumors and was the one who told me that I might have to be a little more direct about my problem if I wanted you to help me have a baby?"

"So *she* gave you that advice, huh? I'll have to thank her for giving me my future."

"I'd love to ask her to the wedding if that's all right with you."

"That sounds great, but do you realize that I haven't met your mother yet, and I was also thinking we might drive over to the Reynolds, one of these days, and see how Claude and Gladys are doing. Maybe let them in on our plans?"

"Oh, Dan, that would be wonderful. With Glenn up in Fort Collins, they probably get quite lonely without any family around although they have a lot of friends at the church, and they belong to a group that calls itself The Nifty Plus Fifty, I think," she giggled. "I see in the bulletin on Sundays that they seem to have a lot of programs to keep them busy. About my mother, I guess I forgot to tell you that she won a trip to St. Thomas and will be gone for five more days. She was so thrilled because she could take someone with her, and she decided to take the man along that she has been dating for the last three years. I have no idea why they have put off getting married."

"Man, you've kept all kinds of news in that sweet head

of yours haven't you? You apparently thought I wouldn't be interested."

"I'm sorry, Dan, but up until yesterday I wasn't sure what to believe where you were concerned. As I told you then, I felt like I was Cinderella, but I didn't know when 12 o'clock was going to chime."

"I'm the one who should be sorry. To let you think I didn't really care, when I was so very much in love with you, was not very considerate of me. Forgive me, Sweetie, because you'll never have to wonder again what my intentions are. I'm just so glad I finally got the chance to propose to you even though you'd only wanted help from my body," he chuckled.

"Maybe we could forget that part of our relationship, Dan. That was one of the most embarrassing moments of my life, and I really would like to erase it from our past."

"Oh, Mauni, that is one of the sweetest memories I'm going to tuck away so that one day I can tell my children and grandchildren how I got to propose to their lovely mother and grandmother," he chuckled but only got a scowling look in return.

Glancing at his watch, he jumped up from the couch and announced that it was time to start getting ready for the big night out. "Do you have everything you'll need, Sweetie, or do you want me to run to the drug store for you? There's one right down the street, if you need anything at all."

"No, Dan, I'm sure I brought everything I'll need. I'm just so excited to be going to Anwan's Restaurant. I've never been there, and I hear it is so eloquent. How did you think to go there, anyway? You really haven't been the hermit everyone thought you were, have you, Dr. Wilder?"

"I'll tell you all about it later, Sweetheart. Right now, you scoot into your bedroom and get all prettied up, although you look gorgeous to me just the way you are."

CHAPTER SEVENTEEN

Monica received an approving whistle from Dan when she emerged wearing a black silk sundress with scattered pearl-sized white dots. The wide halter straps were connected behind the neck, leaving a small area of her back bare. The bodice was fitted to the waist and then the billowy bias-cut skirt fell just to her knees. The 3" heels on her strap sandals made her a vision causing Dan to quickly take her in his arms for a hug. He could hardly wait for her reaction at the restaurant when he could begin his surprise evening.

He had almost rented a tux for the evening but had settled for his one dark designer suit that he'd had custom made after he'd started working, just in case he would need it for a special occasion. He'd only worn it once so it still looked like new. His white shirt and a subdued gray tie made him look very handsome and distinguished.

The restaurant was exquisite with its ornate carvings

in the walnut trim on the chairs and booths, and also on the crown moldings and the chair rails. The thick upholstered seats and backs of the chairs and booths were made of a plush leather. As the maitre' d welcomed them, he shook Dan's hand and winked.

Dan turned to Monica and said, "Honey, this is Nick Oldsberg, a friend from our long ago college days. We sort of got reacquainted about eighteen months ago when I had to do an emergency surgery on him. He's helping make this a special night for us. Nick, this is the Monica Reynolds I told you about."

"Hello, Mr. Oldsberg, it's nice to meet you, I think. I was rather afraid of what Dan had planned for tonight, but now learning that there were actually two of you in on the plan, I'm in complete shock," she giggled.

"No need to worry, Monica, we'll be on our best behavior. Welcome to Anwan's."

On their way to an alcove at one end of the room, Nick whispered in her ear, "Any friend of Dan's is a friend of mine, and we should be on first name basis, so please call me Nick." There were four enclosed booths placed with a window area in between each one. A table, with a beautiful bouquet of flowers, adorned each of those areas and provided extra privacy for the diners. The booths themselves were shaped like a half-circle so you could either sit next to, or across from, one another. Three sides are enclosed up to the lowered ceiling of the alcove, and the open side has light-weight draperies that can be drawn if more privacy is wanted. As they approached, Monica noticed that one server was standing at attention, and only when Nick nodded did he turn and hurry away. She was completely in awe of the splendid service that was given.

A candle, in a lovely etched hurricane globe, provided soft shadows on the table that she noticed had a single long-stemmed rose lying on a white runner. A twinkle, reminding her of a star in the sky, was dancing on the ribbon encircling the rose, but Dan urged her into the booth and took his place opposite her. She could hardly keep her eyes off the rose plus the lovely images made by the candle's flame, and she was wondering if all patrons received a beautiful rose just for eating here. Above all, though, she wanted to keep her eyes on this Dr. Dan Wilder. What exactly did he have planned for tonight?

Dan finally picked up the rose as the server returned and placed two glasses of white wine and a tray of hors d'oeuvres, which looked scrumptious, in the center of their table. Her attention, however, was suddenly drawn to the man approaching them with a big smile on his face. He began to sing directly to her and was accompanied by a Casio back on stage.

> The day I saw you standing there,
> I knew God was by my side,

And if my faith could be strong enough,
You would someday be my bride.
With sunlight shining in your eyes,
Or the moonlight on your face,
For me to find someone as sweet as you,
I had relied upon His grace.

Not by chance or a human scheme,
Only God's hand holding fast
To His plan for you and me, My Love,
As we shared what was our past.

When he'd finished, he smiled and said, "May God's blessings be with you in the life you are planning together." He returned to the stage where the group continued to entertain.

Monica glanced at Dan who was smiling that infectious smile of his and still holding the long-stemmed rose. He reached for her hand and placed the rose across her palm, and when she looked at him and then again at the rose, she realized that the twinkle she had seen was a diamond ring. "Oh, oh, Dan, it's, it's beautiful. How in the world did you get all this planned in less than 24 hours?"

"I had a lot of help from Nick, and not just for tonight. He is a wonderful Christian, Monica, and he tried to get me to go to church with him while we were in college. I wasn't having anything to do with religion at that time, but he said he would keep praying for me. Lucky for me, I met another Christian during my internship, and I finally got my head on straight and became a Christian myself. Nick was really glad to hear that when he'd had to have surgery for the ruptured appendix and I was the surgeon on duty."

"Dan, will you please stop talking and get this ring off the bow and onto my finger? I'm just so excited my fingers won't work." Of course, it was a very simple process when you knew the secret, and apparently Dan had watched closely while it was being put on. He took the ring and slipped around so he was sitting beside her. Then he held her hand, and as he kissed each of her left hand fingers, he was bringing the ring closer to the correct one. When he finally slipped it on, it fit perfectly. She was so dazzled with the size and also the brilliance that she'd almost forgotten where she was, but she had to kiss her man. She didn't care how many were watching, and Dan didn't seem to be disturbed either, and they enjoyed a very long and endearing kiss.

They laughed as they looked at those marvelous hors d'oeuvres and decided they had better indulge before they came and took them away. There were large mushrooms, some filled with crabmeat and some with flavored cream cheese topped with a small slice of fresh strawberry or a dab of blueberries. At each end of the tray were small pieces of celery filled with swirled cheese and garnished with a small piece of pimento or red pepper and a tiny twig of parsley. They were delicious, and the lovebirds realized that they had gotten quite hungry. Dan had pre-ordered Salmon as the main course, served with a rice pilaf, steamed vegetables, and a fresh, crispy salad. Everything had been done to perfection.

Before dessert was served, Dan had taken her, with his hand to the small of her back, and proceeded to the dance floor. They had danced slowly, cheek to cheek, to several of the wonderful old dance tunes that the guys had started playing when they'd seen them coming. Returning to their table, they enjoyed the yummy white cake topped with hot fudge, almonds and cherries, and they had ordered coffee to go with it.

As they were leaving, Nick came over to them with the other eleven roses in a long white box. He handed the box to Dan and then cupped Monica's chin in his hand and kissed her gently on the lips. "You are lovely, Monica, and I can see why Dan has chosen you for his bride. You're also getting a great guy, and I'm hoping my wife and I can get to know you in the years to come. May God bless your marriage!"

Monica had been taken by surprise, but responded

with a hug as he pulled her into a strong embrace. "Maybe you could attend the wedding," she said hesitantly as she realized, too late, that should've been Dan's option. Dan quickly agreed, however, with a sly wink to Nick, and then said he'd let him know the details when they were finalized. Nick, of course, had already been asked to be the groomsman at the wedding.

It was after 10 o'clock when they got back to his apartment and he asked if she could stay overnight. "Dan, I really think I should go on home. I need to be there for the horses in the morning and then get to work on time. Charlotte and Clint do a good job caring for them, but I like to make sure they know I haven't deserted them." She grinned as she realized just how protective she was of those horses, hopefully like she'll be with her children one day.

"O.K. then, I'll follow you and maybe stay over because I don't have an early surgery or appointment tomorrow. How would that set with you, my newly engaged sweetheart?"

"You're going to spoil me rotten, Dr. Wilder, but I'm not going to complain one bit. I'll get my things while you grab a change of clothes, and let's be on our way. I definitely do need my beauty sleep, you know, if I'm going to keep my future husband from wandering."

"You're so funny," he mumbled as he pulled her into

his arms and gave her a quick kiss. "I think I'm the one who'll have to keep an eye on you after that display of attentiveness you gave Nick earlier." He smiled as he kissed the tip of her nose and dashed off to his room to get what he would need to take along.

CHAPTER EIGHTEEN

Monica could hardly wait to get to work the next morning so she could share all her latest news with Trudy and Ann. Of course, they were both ecstatic and so happy for her, but hated the thought of possibly losing her as a fellow nurse so soon. "It's not really fair," Trudy sort of complained, "that you may have to give up your dream of a nursing career. However, we've come to realize that just the possibility of having a child or two of your own, to hold and care for, was something you'd be willing to sacrifice almost anything for. We also knew it had to take precedence over anything else because of your condition. It's possible you'll know more about that this afternoon, though. Of course, when you got to add our handsome Dr. Dan Wilder to the package, why wouldn't you jump at the chance?"

"I second that speech," Ann laughingly remarked, "and I wish you the very best. But, we have patients to care for so we'd better get down to business." She quickly gathered up her equipment and was off to see her first patient of the day.

The day passed rather quickly for Monica because several new patients had been admitted. With vitals to be taken and recorded, and making sure each patient had everything he or she needed, time had really slipped by. It was 3 o'clock and her shift was over.

She'd planned to meet Dan at Dr. Moore's office in an hour, so she decided to go to the cafeteria and get a cool drink. As she relaxed, she wondered how Dan had done with the 'To Do' chores she'd left him with this morning. He'd offered to do anything that she needed to have done, since he had two hours before he had to leave for the hospital. So, she'd asked him to water the flowers outside, since it had been so hot and they hadn't had rain for a few days now. Luckily her yard was pretty shady and her plants were hardy, because she hadn't had time to pamper them. She had also asked if he would prune the two bushes near the barn door that had gotten out of control. As she was wondering if there would be any bushes left when he got finished, she must've been smiling because she heard, "And just what is that big smile all about, My Pretty Lady?"

"Dan, what are you doing here? I thought you were going to be tied up until 4 o'clock and maybe be a little late getting to Dr. Moore's office."

"I had a cancellation this afternoon, so I've been tracking you down for the last fifteen or twenty minutes. I went to the nurses' station, and then I checked to see if your car was still in the lot, which it was, so I thought maybe you were hot and thirsty and had come here. I'm a pretty good detective, don't you think?" He'd slipped in beside her and given her a quick peck on the cheek. "How did Trudy and Ann take the news?"

"They were very disappointed," she laughed. "They think they'll have to stop oohing and aahing over you, when you pass by, and it won't be as much fun here at work anymore. I told them that they could still make a fuss over you, if they wanted to, because you liked to be the center of attention."

"You did what?" he asked, staring at her and trying to look offended, "What do you mean, I like being the center of attention? Well, I do with you, I must admit, and I guess it'll help keep my ego inflated if I get an ooh and an aah now and then," he chuckled. "Do I still have time to get a glass of tea or should we be going?"

"We have plenty of time so go get yourself something. I have at least half of mine to drink yet."

⤚

The doctor's office was empty when they arrived, and the receptionist sighed as her eyes wandered from Dan's head to his toes. She quickly realized who he was with, however, and knew he was definitely out of reach. She dutifully glanced at Monica and made it known that the doctor was with her last patient of the day and would be with them shortly. She tried to concentrate on the reports on her desk, but her eyes kept glancing over to where Dan was checking out the magazines.

Monica could barely hold back the giggles so she kept her back to the receptionist as she picked up a magazine and walked to a chair. Dan was still searching for a magazine to look at, from the selection of ones strictly for women's interests, when the door opened to the examining rooms and Dr. Moore emerged. With a smile on her face, she asked them to come on back. She turned to the receptionist to tell her that she could close the office and then led them to a small conference room.

"Well, now," she said, "it appears things happen pretty quickly when the two of you set your minds to something." She smiled at Monica, remembering her remark on Tuesday about maybe being able to figure out something that might work, but then she turned to Dan. "And, Dr. Wilder, from the rumors I've heard circulating around the hospital for the last two or three years, you were supposed to be the most untouchable of the male breed." Her light blue eyes were twinkling as she glanced at him. "There are quite a few young women, I'm pretty sure, who would love to know Monica's secret that caught your eye. Any clues I can pass on?"

"I really think God had something to do with this miracle, Dr. Moore. I'd thought I was pretty much destined for a solitary life until I caught a glimpse of this one and couldn't let her go."

"That's very possible, Dr. Wilder. God does work in mysterious ways. So, shall we get down to the situation the two of you are most interested in now? I have read several studies on endometriosis and there are no clear rules, or even a suggestion, on the best way to proceed with a dilemma of whether a woman should work or not after she's married. I'll give you the benefit of my own experience as I've followed the progress of five of my more recent patients who had the condition, such as the decisions they made and the outcome of each. I do feel that yours is unique in a way because of the short time Monica and Terry had together before he left for Iraq. That would've been a stressful experience, and I've always felt that stress plays an important role in any pregnancy. That's only my personal opinion, however.

I had two couples in their early or middle thirties who, to me, were still considered newlyweds. When the wives were diagnosed with endometriosis, they decided not to work any longer because they wanted to give themselves every chance to have a baby. Both were pregnant within four or five months. I had another patient, who had been diagnosed with endometriosis about a year before her marriage. She decided to work for at least six more months because they had a few debts that they wanted to get paid off, but, if she didn't get pregnant within the time frame she and her husband had agreed on, she would then quit her job. Well, nothing had happened by the end of the six months so she quit work and then was pregnant about three months later. They now have two little ones and no surgery as yet.

The other two had been married for a few years before being diagnosed. In fact, one had a child about six years old, but this was her second marriage and they wanted to have a child together. Because she felt that she needed to continue working for financial reasons, I prescribed a medication. She did get pregnant and then quit her job because of problems she started having. She had the baby, although prematurely, and then had to have surgery. The baby did survive and is doing fine.

The other one, after getting the diagnosis, did everything I suggested, including not working for awhile, but still hadn't gotten pregnant. She went for another opinion, possibly liked the other doctor and continued working with him. The last I heard, she'd taken another job but is now divorced. She hasn't been back to see me.

I think that gives you my limited knowledge on

this particular matter, but, of course, it's your decision to make." She stood and shook hands as she smiled at them both. "I have to run--the babysitter informed me this morning that she has an important appointment this afternoon, but I sincerely hope yours will be a marriage full of love, commitment, and also the babies I know Monica wants so badly. I wish you both the best and hope you'll keep me posted."

They both uttered softly, "Thank you, we will," as she left the room, but Dan thought he'd seen a look of concern in her eyes as she'd passed by. He didn't know if it was because of Monica's particular condition or not, but that had told him all he needed to know. His wife was not going to be working after the wedding, but he'd let her tell him so it would definitely be her decision.

Monica's eyes were sparkling when they reached his car that they had driven over to the doctor's office. She looked at him and smiled as he opened the door for her and then he hurried around to his side and got in. "Dan, from the look on that 'told you so' face of yours, you knew what her suggestion was going to be all along, didn't you? I think I did, too, but I've enjoyed my job at the hospital more than I ever dreamed I could, and I just couldn't make that decision without more information and my doctor's opinion. I could've just taken your remarks the other night, but I might've always wondered if I was missing something that I wouldn't have needed to. Even worse, I could've come to blaming you. But, I've just been thinking that I could stay involved a little by visiting some of the patients, like our sweet Liz Becker does. I could do that on my own schedule. What would you think about that?"

"I think that sounds like a great idea, Mauni. I know the patients would be thrilled to have you in their lives, and it will keep you in touch with the happenings around the hospital. Plus, you can keep your eagle eye on me." Chuckling, he acted as if he were ducking from a sure punch, and then he asked, "Now, do I get to come out and take a ride with you tonight or do you have other plans?"

Laughing, she said, "You're always ready to change the subject, aren't you, when it concerns something you want to do. I have to call Charlotte and Prudence tonight or they won't speak to me for weeks, but I think I can squeeze in a ride with you. Tumbleweed and Rascal will be thrilled to get away from the barn and into the shade of the trees plus a cool drink from the pond. Are you going to your apartment first or do you have clothes in the trunk of your car again? You'd better bring more than one change, just in case you should slip into the pond. It would be purely accidental, of course."

"You little devil, you're asking for a little dunking

yourself, it seems, so I'll come prepared for anything. Here's your car. Why don't you come to the apartment while I get my things, and then I can follow you on home?"

"Right with you, My Lord," she giggled as she quickly scooted out of the car, when he'd opened the door, and then jumped into hers before he realized what she was up to. She just grinned and made a face at him as she started her car and pulled away. He scurried back around to get into his own but then took a moment to just think and pray.

Never a dull moment with that one, but I wouldn't want it any other way. "Thank you, Lord, for filling my life with this precious woman, and may I always be worthy of her love. Help me to accept all that she has to offer, and to never try to change her in my quest for a perfect marriage. I'm afraid at times, Lord, that I may not have the patience, since I've been alone for so long. That means I'll need your guidance so I don't make too many big mistakes. I have to realize that there will be differences, and as Monica has told me--when that happens, we'll just work them out. You've brought her into my life, and I'll do my best to make her content and happy. Amen."

Her car wasn't in front of his apartment when he arrived, and his poor stomach started turning flip flops. He was sure she would've remembered how to get here, and he would've seen her car along the way if she'd had trouble. *Where can she be?* he pondered as he got out of his car and glanced down the street. The traffic was getting heavier as it was now after 5 o'clock and everyone was heading home from work. *What should I do now?* he wondered as his hands were clammy and his heart was beating like a trotting horse.

Just then he thought he saw her car turn onto his street about two blocks away. *How could she have made a wrong turn there? That's a dead end street right beside a gas station. Oh, I guess it's going to take me awhile to get used to being married, especially to this very independent woman.* He hurried to unlock the door so he could try to act unconcerned when she arrived.

"I didn't realize I was running on empty until I was almost here," she rather casually remarked as she walked in the door. "I guess I'll have to invest in a cell phone so I can let you know where I am. I saw you go by the station and tried to get your attention, but your eyes were looking straight ahead."

"And I guess that means I'll have to learn to look to the right, to the left, and straight ahead, all at once, to keep track of you," he retorted.

Grinning, she came and put her arms around his waist and gave him a tight squeeze. "You weren't worried about me, were you, Darlin'? I could see you standing by your car and looking down the street. I'm so sorry if I caused you to worry," she said playfully. She then reached up and put her arms around his neck and gave him a very reassuring kiss.

"I don't know what I'm going to do with you, Mauni, but I'm very sure that I can't live without you." He held her tight and he couldn't have felt any more content.

During their ride later in the twilight hours, they'd tried to come up with an unusual way to announce their engagement to family and close friends. Several ideas were discussed, but they were voted down until finally they'd thought about having a spur-of-the-moment cookout which sounded great to them both. They'd wait until everyone finished eating and then make it a surprise announcement. That became their final plan.

The following week was busy for both of them, not only at the hospital, but also as they made sure all the details were taken care of for the cookout they had planned for Sunday evening, August 14th.

CHAPTER NINETEEN

Dan hadn't forgotten his promise to Neil and Susan, either, and he had been in contact with Dr. Charles Noland, a wonderful doctor whom he had known since his teenage days in the little town of Hayes. The doctor seemed very interested in meeting Neil and said he'd be happy to discuss the possibility of a position in his office. "The town just keeps growing," he had said to Dan, "but no one seems to want to come here to be a doctor. I'm not quite ready to retire yet, but I'd sure like a day off now and then." So, Dan had made the arrangements to meet Neil at the North Side Mall on Saturday morning, the 13th, and then he would drive from there.

When Dan and Monica had finished what had become their favorite Friday night ride, they talked a little more about the cookout Sunday night. They had both extended invitations by phone, but they'd decided they wouldn't tell any of them that it was going to be the formal announcement of their engagement. "I'll find out for sure tomorrow, while I'm in Hayes with Neil, if Tim and Kate are going to get to come," Dan remarked as they discussed the doubtful ones. "I know that Nick and his wife are planning to be here unless an emergency occurs at the restaurant. Oh, I just had a thought, Mauni. Should I ask Neil if he and Susan would like to drive down?"

"That would be wonderful, Dan. I'm really glad you thought of it. Did I tell you that my brother Drew called? He said he'd been wanting to come down to see Mom and me, and this was a perfect time for him. When I stopped to see Claude and Gladys, I don't remember them being as excited when Terry and I were married as they are about this get together, and *that* Gladys was the only one who wouldn't accept that it was just a potluck. She twisted my arm until I had to admit that it was a very special occasion, but I wasn't going to tell her who the honorees were. She just looked at me, grinned, and then very quietly said, *'We'll see, but my intuitions are usually right'.*" Giggling, Monica could only shake her head in disbelief. "They were going to call Glenn and urge him to come home for a long weekend because she is so sure it has something to do with you and me. Drew and Glenn, both being professors, have some time left before the fall term begins.

And, I'll actually get to go to the morning service

Sunday, since I have the day off, so I'll get Pastor Haskell
aside and ask if he and the church would be available for
a small, but very important, wedding on September 2. If
they are, we can announce that at the cookout, too. Oh,
Dan, it doesn't seem possible that this is happening to me.
I couldn't be happier."

"Let's take a few minutes here and bring me up to date
on a couple of things. First, you have never mentioned
your maiden name, so I'm at a loss to know how to address
your brother, Drew, or your mother, for that matter. Also,
you mentioned that Drew had been wanting to come
down to see your mother and you, but I thought your
mother was on that cruise for three more days. Is Drew
staying for a few extra days to see her? Answers, My Dear,
I need answers," he chuckled.

Monica started laughing and trying to talk at the same
time. Dan couldn't understand a word she was saying, so
he took her in his arms and kissed her. That wasn't the
least bit successful, however, because when the kiss ended,
she started laughing even harder. He then just leaned back
on the couch and waited.

Finally, she was calm again and proceeded to give him
the answers to his inquiries. "My brother's name is Drew
Morgan, a professor at U of C, Boulder. Glenn Reynolds,
the brother of Terry, is also a professor but at Colorado
State in Fort Collins. Now, about my dear mother, Mona

Morgan. She just sent Drew and me an e-mail saying the cruise had been cut short by three days because of some trouble with the ship, and they had to bring it back to port. She and Keith Cormann will be home tomorrow night, and she said she had a surprise. Isn't it great? They'll be home in time for the cookout."

"Do you suppose we should plan a double wedding?"

"No, September 2 is to be "our day" and I want it to be just that. If that *is* her big surprise, and she is engaged or maybe already married, I'll be thrilled for her, but it's not going to interfere with our wedding day."

"I was hoping you would feel that way, but I didn't want to appear selfish if you and your mother would like to be married in a double ceremony."

"Well, it's not going to happen, so that's that. I don't think Mom would go for it either, but what about your parents? Were you able to reach them?"

"Not yet. It appears they are traveling somewhere in Europe and won't return until August 20th. I talked to the maid and she promised to tell them I'd called, and I told her I'd try to call again on Sunday, the 21st. They'll still have time to fly up here if they want to see their only son get married. I'm not going to hold my breath, though."

"Oh, Dan, I'm so sorry. I did tell you, didn't I, that I

want to see if Drew can be here to give me away? He was so disappointed, when Terry and I were married, that he couldn't even get here, so I definitely want him beside me this time."

"I hope, with all my heart, that wish comes true, Sweetheart, but now, if everything is under control, I think I'll head home and get ready to meet Neil in the morning. You said you had to talk to Charlotte and Prudence tonight, so I'll give you some space."

After a big hug and a goodnight kiss, Dan was out the door and heading home. All of his thoughts were on the wedding. *There are just three more weeks before September 2, and so much yet to do. Well, ready or not, on that Friday, God willing, we'll be married and then we'll begin our life together. I should've suggested an earlier date because I can hardly wait.*

Saturday morning, Dan found Neil waiting at the Mall. They got some fresh coffee to take with them, and then they were on their way. Dan could tell that Neil was so excited he could hardly sit still. He turned on some music, hoping it might calm him a little, and he did seem to relax. During a couple songs, Dan heard him singing along in a great baritone voice. "Hey, Neil, I hope you use that voice for more than a lullaby for that little boy of yours."

"Susan and I used to sing together in the choir at our church and it was actually where we realized we loved each other. After we were married, it seemed like so many things were happening, and then the lay-off, that choir practice was out of the question. In fact, we were lucky to make it to the one church service some weeks."

"Well, if it works out for you down here in Hayes, I think you'll have time to get into a choir again. Dr. Noland is a wonderful Christian, and only in the case of a dire emergency would he miss Sunday services. The Community Church is the one that the original settlers had started, and it is still going strong. The Hayes family attends there, and anything that is anything in Hayes, that family most likely had a hand in it. They are wonderful people, very friendly, so generous to everyone, and I know you'll love getting acquainted with them."

Dan had deliberately gone to the second exit into Hayes so, as they drove toward the town, he could pass the Haven of Rest Ranch, which is owned by the Hayes family. When they reached the actual town, there was the old historic Broad Street Hotel to admire along with some of the other stores along Main Street. Finally, there was the Hayes Law Firm and Jeremiah Park. He then turned right, or south, onto Lakeland Drive to Lincoln Blvd. where he turned right again to point out the historic Community Church and the Court House, each situated in a full block along a beautifully landscaped boulevard. He was surprised, however, to see the impressive Retirement Center across from the church and also the two-story Clinic across from the court house that Tim had told him about. They were certainly outstanding additions to the town. Turning north onto South Broad Street, he pointed out the high school on the left and also the library farther north on the right side of the street. He then pulled up in front of a nice one story brick building with a sign indicating that they had reached the office of Dr. Charles Noland.

"This building was built about ten years ago and it was, at that time, equipped with all the newest medical equipment that was available. Knowing Dr. Noland, I would bet that the latest inventions since then have also been added," Dan explained. "Behind here you'll find a drug store, and behind the library is the City Hall and the Post Office. So, Neil, what do you think of the little town so far?"

"It appears that the little town has everything a family would probably need. It's quite different from Denver, but it is a lot like the little town I worked in before with Dr. Brady. I like what I've seen so far because it will be a wonderful place to raise children, and it appears to be a place you can feel your family will be safe."

"I think we're right on time, which will please the

Doc because he sort of frowns on wasting time. So shall we go? He's a great guy, so don't be nervous. Just answer all of the questions you can, and if he tries to throw you a curve, just smile. He can be a little devious at times, but smarter than most city doctors. You normally have to be when you're the only doctor within 15 or 20 miles."

When they reached the door, it flew open and Dr. Noland stood straight and tall in his white jacket, a stethoscope around his neck, and a big smile on his face. "Come in, come in," he said as he extended his hand to Dan and then to Neil. "So, you're Neil Davis, the young doctor who tried to farm when he couldn't find a medical job. Well, let's see if we might be able to remedy that." He led them into his office, after telling his nurse that he didn't want to be disturbed unless. . .of course, she knew the rules.

His office was a light, cheery room with a large mahogany desk, a nice leather swivel chair, and three leather side chairs which faced the desk. When they were all seated, he then addressed Neil with a smile. "Dan gave me the little bit of information he had on you, Neil, but I could feel that he had been quite impressed. I hope you don't mind, but I called and talked to Dr. Brady, whom I've known since we were in our residency together, and he was also quite complementary and so glad you were getting an opportunity to continue in the medical field."

"Thank you, Sir. Dr. Brady was wonderful to me and I really learned a tremendous amount of valuable medical procedures from him."

"I'm sure you did because he was one of the top achievers in our class. Of course, I just happened to be the other one," he chuckled and then continued to ask questions as he showed them around, including the examining rooms, a small x-ray room, a lab and other areas of a doctor's office, such as the patients' files, the supply room and the computer set-up.

Neil had a few questions of his own which seemed to please Dr. Noland as they had again reached his office.

After the interview was over, Dan was so impressed with Neil that he wished he could have him working beside him at the hospital in Colorado Springs, but this little town, with Dr. Noland as his mentor, was just what God would want for this talented young man and his family.

Dan could tell that the doctor was also impressed and wasn't surprised when Neil had been offered a position as soon as he could get his family moved and settled. Sensing that a miracle had already happened for Neil this morning, it was hard to believe when another was offered. Dr. Noland said, "Neil, there's a house here in town that belonged to my grandson and his wife, before they decided to go to the mission field, and it is sitting unoccupied, but furnished. They needed money to fund their mission, and time was too short to try to sell the house before they were to leave, so I bought it from them. I understand you lost all or most of your possessions in the fire, so if you are interested in looking at it, I'll be glad to show it to you. You can rent it very reasonably, with the option to buy later if you decide you'd like to do that, and the first month's rent is free."

Neil had tears in his eyes as he replied, "I don't know what to say, Dr. Noland. When I learned that it was Dr. Wilder and Monica who had come to our rescue the day of the fire, I thought that was a real miracle. Then he offered to help me find a job, and that was a miracle too good to even contemplate. As busy as I knew he was, I guess I was a little surprised that he didn't walk away and forget his promise, like so many do. And now, I feel as if two more miracles have happened today. I just wish Susie were here to share all this joy right now that I'm feeling. I'd be thrilled to look at the house, Dr. Noland, and then we could be moved in and ready to help you so much sooner."

"Well, Son, I really appreciate your coming into my life, and I already feel that I can take an afternoon off and not worry about the patients. And, we must remember that none of it would've happened without Dan being the compassionate man that he is, and that God was also looking over all of us." Church attendance had also been one of the topics of discussion during the interview, and Dan had advised Dr. Noland of the fact that Neil and Susan had both sung in the choir at their church. He couldn't vouch for Susan's voice, but he certainly knew that Neil was a very outstanding baritone.

"That will be looked into when they get settled and become acquainted with some of the people around town," Dr. Noland affirmed. "Christy Hayes and Jon Holcomb are both in the choir and they sing so beautifully together. Of course, they'll be getting married soon. I believe I heard that it would be in October. They would be a wonderful couple to get to know, and we can always use good singers in the choir."

The house was a large one-story bungalow with three bedrooms downstairs, a small attic room with a dormer window on the second floor, and a full finished basement. It was perfect, Neil thought, because Susie had become so afraid of second floors in any home since the fire when she'd been caught upstairs with the baby.

After everything was settled, Dan and Neil found Tim to confirm his coming to the cookout. Dan showed Neil some more of the town which included the home where he had grown up. It was to the east of Lakeland Drive and south on Wilder Road, of course. It had been named back when his dad bought the land and built the house. They then headed north on Lakeland Drive to the highway and back toward Colorado Springs. On the way, Dan had asked Neil if he thought he and Susan could possibly come down for the cookout tomorrow night. When he told him there was going to be a special announcement, Neil, expecting it to be a wedding announcement, immediately said that they would be there. Dan gave him the final directions before they parted.

It had been a fun day, and such a rewarding one to see two exceptional men receive a gift of life, so to speak, because Neil could now become the doctor he had studied so hard to achieve, and Dr. Noland could finally relax a little and enjoy time away from the office.

Dan could hardly wait to get to Monica's so she could hear the wonderful news about Neil and Dr. Noland. He wasn't prepared, however, for the hysterical state that he found her in when he walked into the house. He finally got her to tell him that she had heard on the TV news that a helicopter had gone down in the gulf. It was while they were flying persons back to the mainland who had been stranded on a crippled ship that was trying to get back to port. There were no reports yet on survivors or if there were any casualties.

He sat and held her, not knowing what words would or could console her if anything should happen to her mother who had struggled so hard to raise her and her brother without much help from the father. He caressed her arms that were so cold, and kissed the top of her head, her cheeks and her lips, trying to comfort her in this anxiety of not knowing. It seemed like they'd sat there for hours, the TV repeating over and over that there were no reports yet of the people who had been on the helicopter.

He was a little startled when the phone rang, but he managed to untangle her arms from around him and reach the phone. There was a crackling noise and then he heard a faint voice. He listened very closely but could only hear, "We are OK, Monica. We are OK." He tried to talk to them, but they apparently couldn't hear his voice, but again he heard, "Please don't worry, Monica, we are OK," and then the click of the phone being shut off. Coming back to sit down beside Monica, he took her in his arms and conveyed the message as best he could, but she was like a limp rag doll curled up on the couch. "Honey, did you hear what I said? They are OK and they said for you not to worry. I think her phone might have been a little weak because the reception wasn't too clear, but I heard her say that they were OK and for you not to worry loud and clear."

"How do I know it was really them?" she asked as her sobbing began again.

"Because they said your name twice, Sweetie, and

they also said, 'We are OK, and don't worry, Monica, we're OK.' Now, you have to believe and try to be strong. You don't want them coming home to find you a basket case when they let you know that they're OK. Please, Sweetheart, let's thank God that He is with them and has kept them safe."

Monica looked up at him and smiled. "You're right, as always. God is with them and they did call to let us know that they are safe. I was so afraid, Dan, for Mom first and then I got to thinking about you and Neil out on the highway. I couldn't imagine what I would do if something happened to you, and I really got hysterical. I'm so sorry." She curled up in his arms and was soon sound asleep, completely exhausted.

CHAPTER TWENTY

Monica slept in Dan's arms for almost an hour, and she awoke calm but apologetic for being such a worrier. After she'd freshened up a bit and he'd changed into shorts and a polo shirt, they drove to the Mall and got a bite to eat. They discussed his day with Neil, the time with Dr. Noland, her day at work, and the final details on the cookout.

He'd offered to go to church with her tomorrow so he could meet the pastor when she planned to talk to him following the service. Since they dress casually during the hot days of summer, the slacks and shirt he'd worn today would be fine.

When they'd returned from the Mall, they had taken a short ride before feeding the horses, and then relaxed to watch a movie on DVD. At a very interesting part of the show, the phone rang. It was almost 11 o'clock and Monica tensed up again, so Dan answered it again. It was her mother, so Monica jumped up and quickly took the phone from him.

"Oh, Mom, I was so worried when I saw the news on the TV. I was here by myself because Dan was out of town, and I was a basket case when he came by to tell me about his day. And then we got your call, but you apparently couldn't hear us and Dan had to convince me that God was watching over you and keeping you safe." She rattled on until Dan touched her arm and whispered that she should let her mother talk. "Oh, I'm sorry, Mom, where are you, and are you and Keith really OK?"

"I was beginning to wonder if I was going to be able to get a word in," she laughed. "Yes, Sweetie, Keith and I are both fine, and we just arrived at his apartment. We had also heard about the helicopter accident and that is why we called. We were in the Dallas airport, but my cell phone was losing power. We are absolutely beat, but I wanted to let you know that we're home and will be at the cookout tomorrow night. By the way, who is this Dan that I assume answered the phone just now, and also earlier? You aren't holding out on me, are you, Monica?"

"You'll have to be at the cookout to find out anything more, Mother, so I'll see you both tomorrow. Get a good night's rest, and I'm so glad you're home safe and sound. I love you so much, and I'm looking forward to seeing you at 6:30 tomorrow. Bye now." She then broke the connection before her mother could ask any more questions, but she turned toward Dan and frowned when she heard him chuckling. "I just want our announcement to be a big surprise tomorrow night," she scowled. "Hey, I just realized that Mom didn't even mention her big surprise. I wonder what it's going to be. I think ours will be a bigger surprise to her than hers will be to us," she giggled. She settled quickly into Dan's arms, but had to give him a sweet, tender kiss before resuming the movie.

Sunday morning was busy with chores, a big breakfast, and getting ready for church. The service was very inspiring, as Dan felt that Pastor Haskell was a very good speaker, and the choir's anthem was beautiful. Monica and Dan waited around until the congregation had pretty well disbanded, and then approached the pastor. "Could we speak to you for just a few minutes, Pastor Haskell? This is Dr. Dan Wilder, my fiance'," she smiled as she showed him her ring. "We'd like to reserve the church and your services on September 2, if possible."

"Let's go to my office where we can continue this conversation in private," and as he started off down the hall, he was grinning. He looked over at her and very quietly remarked, "Well, now, you go and get yourself a job at the hospital and within a month or two, you're engaged to a handsome young doctor. That's pretty fast work, Monica." He was chuckling all the way to his very nice and comfortable office. After the three of them were seated, he then asked, "Do either of you want to elaborate on the suddenness of this, or may I assume it has something to do with Monica's waning health problem? She has, by the way, discussed that with me, Dr. Wilder."

"The reason for our wanting to get married, Sir, is that we are absolutely crazy about each other. I was so captivated by her that I would've married her the day I met her, but she kept hiding from me." He grinned and winked at Monica. "The suddenness is, as you have assumed, the fact that she got word from her gynecologist recently that time is running out for her to successfully conceive and carry a child. Therefore, we'd like to be married as soon as possible so we can begin trying to give her the baby she wants so desperately."

"I'm so happy that you have found each other, understand the circumstances, and now need a wedding to take place. You mentioned September 2, didn't you?" He then flipped his calendar from August to September, glanced at it a second, and said, "You two are in luck. My calendar is clear for that day so are you wanting an afternoon or an evening ceremony?"

Monica spoke up, "Would 7 o'clock be all right with you? Some of our guests work, so that would give them time to get here."

"That's fine. I'll put it on the calendar right now. Are you going to want the organist, a singer, or anything I can help with, or will it just be you and a few guests?"

"If it would be all right, Pastor Haskell, I have a friend who was going to provide the music. He'll arrange to have a singer, with his own accompaniment." Dan looked at Monica to see what her reaction was going to be to this bombshell, but she was smiling as tears were running down her cheeks. He took that as her approval.

"Do you suppose he'll sing "God By My Side" all the way through?" she whispered to Dan. "I pulled it up on the Internet, and it is so beautiful."

"I think that can be arranged, Sweetheart."

"It sounds like you have things pretty much under control," Pastor Haskell chuckled. "I'd like to meet with you once again for the usual pastor's instructional discussion. Monica has been through it once, but what about you, Dr. Wilder?"

"This will be my first marriage. I've waited until I was absolutely sure, because I knew God was in my corner. When I saw Monica, He gave me all the tingles and assurances I needed to know that she was the one for me. And, Sir, would you please call me Dan?"

"Thank you, Dan, I appreciate that. Now, could the two of you meet with me right after the Wednesday night service, say about 8 o'clock?"

"We'll be here," they said, almost in unison.

Smiling, the pastor stood, shook their hands, and as he followed them from the room, he said in a soft but audible whisper, "God, I like this one."

❦

It was now just a little past 4:30. Charlotte and Clint had pulled into the drive, and was followed closely by Prudence and Derrick. The four looked rather concerned when Dan wasn't there, but Monica quickly assured them that he would be back shortly.

Fifteen minutes later, Dan's car turned in, followed by one Monica didn't recognize. When the car door opened as Dan approached it, however, she let out a scream and ran to the yard. She had seen it was her brother, Drew, but who was in the car with him? She ran into his outstretched arms and he swung her around and around as he hugged her so tightly she could hardly breathe. "Monica, I wanted to come early because I knew I wouldn't get the chance to tell you my news if Mom got here first. He took her hand and walked around the car to open the door for a very pretty brunette with beautiful brown eyes. She was smiling as she emerged and stood beside Drew. She wore light beige Bermuda shorts, which showed her long shapely legs to perfection, and a carnation pink top accented her tanned skin.

"Darling, this is my little sister, Monica, whom I have

told you so much about. Sis, this is my wife, Diane. We actually eloped four weeks ago, the 16th of July. We had just gotten back from our honeymoon when you called. When you extended the invitation to the cookout today, I decided to wait and surprise you when we got here. I didn't think Mom and Keith would be home yet, but when that changed, I knew she couldn't keep it a secret once she saw you, so we decided to arrive early. Hope it doesn't spoil any of your plans." He'd given her a brotherly wink because he hadn't missed that sparkle radiating between his sister and this nice looking guy he'd just met.

"Drew, you stinker, how could you elope and not let anyone know?" She turned to Diane, and, without hesitation they were hugging as if they had known each other for years. "I'm so happy for the two of you. We'll have to catch up on all the news, but let's go into the house where it's much cooler than here in the afternoon sun. By the way, this is Dan Wilder if he didn't introduce himself before I came running out."

"We did exchange names, but I *am* a little curious about the closeness you two seem to be exhibiting," he chuckled.

Just then the sun porch door opened and Charlotte and Prudence came running out. They couldn't wait any longer to welcome the heart throb of their teenage years and his wife. Clint and Derrick decided they'd better join the reunion, but they all returned shortly to the house and the comfortable air-conditioning.

By 6:30 everyone had arrived, and Monica could see the disappointment in her mom's eyes that she hadn't been able to break the news of Drew's marriage, but she had been thrilled to meet her new daughter-in-law. Mona, however, was definitely wondering about this Dan, who seemed to know his way around the house better than just an acquaintance. *Where did that daughter of mine meet him, and where has she been keeping him? I don't remember even hearing his name until he answered the phone yesterday. I'll admit that I've been gone for three long weeks, but can that look, so obviously love, appear in such a short time? My curiosity is getting the best of me, so someone had better say something soon.*

Claude and Gladys also got quite a surprise when Glenn arrived with a Patty Gray. It was soon discovered that they'd been dating for over three months but he hadn't mentioned it at the time of his dad's hospitalization. He'd whispered to his mother that this might be the one, and Gladys had given him a big hug. Could she possibly be getting another daughter?

The eight younger guys congregated around the grill while the girls were making sure all the rest of the food that had been brought was ready to be taken outside when the steaks were done. Keith and Claude had decided to remain in the house, and they'd found they had a lot in common. Keith is still practicing law, planning to retire in a couple of years, and Claude had retired only two years ago after being seated on the bench for thirty years.

It had cooled down out under the trees by the time the guys announced that the steaks were ready. The girls came out with a relish tray, potato salad and baked beans, a big tossed salad, a bowl of fresh fruit, some homemade cookies, plus the delicious cake that Gladys had baked. Some had contributed to the cost of the steaks. They ate until they were stuffed, and little remained of all the food that had been there to begin with.

Monica had cornered Drew and confided in him all about the wedding and how Dan had tried to talk her into eloping, too. She asked if he thought he could possibly make it this time and give her away. "I wouldn't miss it for the world, Sis, and I want to apologize again for being so self-centered about my career that I didn't make it for you and Terry. I've kicked myself so many times for that blunder."

When things had quieted down a bit from clearing the dishes and getting the few left-overs into the kitchen, Dan stood up and asked to speak. He called Monica to his side, and with his arm around her waist, he began:

"You're probably wondering why, in the heat of August, we've made you suffer at an outdoor cookout.

Some of you had never laid eyes on me before today, some had known me for only a short time, while others have known me for quite a few years or almost all my life. So, again, I'm Dan Wilder, a surgeon at the hospital here in Colorado Springs, and I met this wonderful girl on July 6 when I had a patient I'd had to patch up after being thrown from his horse. Monica was his nurse on her first day of work. I was so captivated, as I listened to her talking to the patient about her loss and the dilemma she was facing, I would've married her that very day, but she had other ideas and kept hiding from me.

I finally had to take some drastic steps just to get to talk to her. First, I blocked her path out of the patient's room. Second, I looked up her name and address in the directory and drove out here just to see where she lived and to possibly get a peek at the horses. Of course, I felt like a fool when I ran into the dead end road and had to turn into her drive. To make things worse, there she was standing right in the yard looking confused, if not angry, having to see me again so soon." Of course, laughter filled the air.

"She was most gracious, however, and even offered me a glass of ice tea and a cookie because I'd had the top down on the car. You can imagine, I'm sure, what my throat felt like, and my car will never be the same. We had a wonderful conversation, a horseback ride, and a great supper together, and over the last six weeks, we've become close friends, confidantes, and, as of last Thursday night, engaged to be married as we are definitely in love."

Monica held up her left hand for all to see her ring.

There was clapping, whistling, and whooping from the group of twenty. "But," Dan held up his hand for silence so he could continue, "we're not only going to announce our engagement tonight, but also the date of our wedding. It is, actually, less than three weeks away, on September 2. Now, before you all gasp and wonder if I've been a very bad boy, I want to explain why we are in such a hurry. Mauni was diagnosed, as some of you know, with endometriosis shortly before Terry was called to go to Iraq. Although they tried to get her pregnant in the very short time they had before he left, it didn't happen, and then she lost Terry a little over a year ago.

Her gynecologist told her recently, after a recurrence of the attacks, she possibly has three or four years, at the most, to still be able to conceive and have a baby before surgery is necessary. This condition is very unpredictable, so, being the generous man that I am, I've offered to be the father of her children, although it had to be as her husband, also. If we're so blessed, we may be able to have at least two little bundles of joy before the surgery has to be performed.

That's our story. The wedding is going to be at the Countryside Christian Church at 7 o'clock on Friday, September 2. A private dinner will follow at Anwan's Restaurant, and if you are unfamiliar with its location, you'll be able to follow the limousine carrying the bride and groom and attendants. You are all hereby invited to attend the festivities, and several of you have been, or will be, asked to be a part of the ceremony.

And now, as any good political speaker would ask, Are there any stupid questions?"

He was laughing as he immediately turned to Monica, took her in his arms and kissed her, totally convincing everyone there that he had meant every word.

CHAPTER TWENTY-ONE

"I honestly don't know how he's accomplished every little detail of the reception with all the surgeries he's had, as well as his regular appointments. He took Neil to Hayes after talking to Dr. Noland on the phone several times, plus his needless worry about me and my condition. He's been smothering me with tender loving care. He was absolutely wonderful when he found me so hysterical about Mom and Keith." Monica was telling Charlotte and Prudence about her marvelous Dan when they met Monday for lunch. They were then going to shop for their wedding dresses.

"Well, however he did it, it sounds scrupulous to the last detail, but do you think there could be others who'll come to the wedding and expect to come to the dinner as well?" asked Prudence. She's the serious one who is always thinking of possible situations that could mess up any well-laid plans.

Ignoring that comment, Charlotte asked, "Do we want to wear short dresses, or do we want to wear long ones, since it's an evening wedding? Also, it's going to be September, if only the 2nd, so the Fall colors would be appropriate, if you'd prefer."

"Gee, Char, you're so good at making me more confused than I already am. What do you have to add, Pru?"

"I'm still thinking about the dinner," she laughed, "but, what would you think about a mid-calf dress for the bride and maybe short ones for the attendants? I'm not so sure about that, though. Maybe they should all be the same length."

"Well, I know one thing for sure, and that is that Dan does *not* want a formal affair. He would have eloped, like Drew, if I had given him any encouragement at all, but he has graciously agreed to the church wedding because he knows that is what I want. So, I will definitely not go against his wishes by being in a formal wedding gown with a train, and then expect him to be in a tuxedo. I'm afraid he just wouldn't show up, and I won't lose him over such a trivial matter."

"Let's go to two or three of the dressier shops and see what we can find. Surely we'll be able to find something that will work," Charlotte announced as she stood to leave.

Nothing had appealed to them in the first shop they'd gone to but, in the second shop, the clerk was very helpful and took them into a room where, she informed them, they kept a special selection of dresses for non-formal weddings. After rejecting the first two matching bride and attendant dresses that the clerk showed them, she then selected one for Monica that Charlotte and Prudence insisted she try on. It looked sensational on her, plus it wouldn't need any alterations. But, Monica wasn't sure she wanted to settle for the first one she'd tried on, so they kept looking. She tried three or four more, all pretty and fit well, but they all, at last, decided the first one was the one to buy.

It wasn't hard for Charlotte and Prudence to pick theirs after the bride was satisfied. With the clerk's expertise, they soon had their dresses and shoes, plus just a puff of a veil to be attached to a darling ringlet of pearls for Monica's head. They left that store elated.

Next was the flower shop. With pictures of the dresses, they found a very helpful bridal consultant who, within a short time, seemed to know just what was needed to go with the dresses. She also was helpful in selecting a simple theme for the front of the church. She suggested entwining flowers through the candelabra she knew the church had, because she'd decorated there before. She'd be there early enough to fix the front of the church and see that all those involved would have appropriate flowers. Monica had included, of course, flowers for Dan's parents, praying that they'd be there for him, as well as Keith and Mona, Drew and Diane, and Claude and Gladys. They'd also decided on the flowers for their bouquets and the guys' boutonnieres. Was that all? If not, she was told she could call through Friday morning, the day of the wedding, to add or deduct.

Monica realized she still had to get a ring, but she'd have to find out the size first, so they called it a day. After all, it was almost 6 o'clock and her two friends had husbands who would be waiting for them. It had been a wonderful, gratifying day. She drove home singing a song while making up a few words of her own. "It was no accident, our love so true, Jesus surely had a hand in it before we even knew." Oh, she was so happy!

Wednesday afternoon, Dan followed her home so they could go for their talk with the pastor. She hadn't seen him since the cookout, but they had talked each night. There were a few things she still wanted to discuss with him before they went to the church.

"Do I get to peek at your dress?" Dan asked as they were cleaning up the dishes after dinner. "I think I should get to approve of it before the wedding. What if I don't like you in it and want to change my mind?"

"Well, my dress is not here, Dan, but if what I look

like in that dress would determine whether you want to marry me or not, you may hit the road, Dr. Wilder, right now." She was standing with her arms crossed in front of her and a scowl on her face. Her stance was one of sheer disgust, but it lasted all of a mere three seconds until he could pull her into an embrace and kiss the frown away.

"You know you could wear a burlap bag and I'd still love looking at you and wanting to marry you, Sweetheart, so don't get upset with me for having a little fun."

"Actually, I like your teasing, but I'm not sure I'm in the mood for it right now with the wedding plans, the meetings, and the 'what have I forgotten' clogging up my mind. There is one thing I want to talk to you about before we see the pastor. Prudence brought up the idea that there may be some who will come to the wedding and then expect to be invited to the dinner afterwards, since we aren't sending out invitations. I was wondering if we should have a small reception at the church before going to the restaurant. What do you think?"

"We are having a 7 o'clock wedding, Mauni, and I think that a private dinner is all we can squeeze into the time we'll have after the small intimate ceremony that I'm hoping this is going to be. Maybe we should have Pastor Haskell put an announcement in the bulletin on the 28th that a private wedding ceremony and dinner for family members and a few close friends will be held

Friday, September 2, uniting Monica M. Reynolds and Dan Wilder. No time will be mentioned and no restaurant name. How's that?"

"As usual, you are the solver of all my problems. We'll ask the pastor not to give out any other information. There's one omission in your statement, though, that I'd like to have in that announcement, and that's Dr. Daniel D. Wilder, not just Dan Wilder. Will you agree to that?"

"Yes, Sweetie, I'll go along with that."

"Did I tell you that I ordered flowers for your father and mother, so we'll have enough if they do get to come? There'll only be the flowers entwined through the candelabra at the front of the church, with the candles burning, during the ceremony. Have you talked to Nick anymore about what the music will be? I was wondering if The Lord's Prayer could be sung while we kneel to pray."

"I have to kneel and pray out loud? What are you getting me into here?"

"No, Dan, you don't pray out loud. We kneel while The Lord's Prayer is sung, which is like a prayer being said, but only in music. Haven't you ever been to a church wedding?"

Grinning, he ran his finger down her cheek and whispered, "Only once or twice, and I wasn't paying much attention to what was going on. I've heard about rehearsals, too--do we need to go through one of those?"

"I don't think so. I don't care how many mistakes we make as long as we say the 'I do's' when we're supposed to, and we're legally married when it's over." He realized she was laughing at him again and he stopped it short with a nice long kiss.

They waited in the narthex for the Wednesday night meeting to be over, and then they went to the Pastor's office. It was a rather short discussion as Pastor Haskell asked about the type of ceremony they preferred, if they were going to kneel to pray, and if they'd planned to light the keepsake unity candle. A few details with the music would have to be worked out, and they would get back with him about those. Otherwise, after the few questions and their answers about the commitment they were entering into, the pastor felt they were definitely well prepared for marriage and the responsibilities that came with it. Then, with a slight grin, he assured them that he would be pleased to officiate at their wedding.

Since Dan had a real early surgery scheduled in the morning, and Monica also had to be at work for the day shift, they said their goodnights quickly and Dan left for home. The house always seems empty now when he leaves, and Monica certainly hopes the next two and a half weeks go by real fast.

৵

Suddenly it was Saturday, the 20th, and Dan's parents were scheduled to get home from their trip abroad today. He'd told the maid that he would call on the 21st, but he was wanting to know their reaction as soon as possible. *What will their answer be when I ask if they can come to my wedding on such short notice? Well, just looking at the phone isn't going to get me any answers.* He was a little apprehensive and even felt his hands getting clammy as he dialed, but when the maid answered his hopes really took a nose dive until she quickly assured him that his parents were home and were waiting for his call.

"Daniel, my boy, how are you?" he heard his father's booming voice come through the line. "We're sure sorry we missed your other call, but what can we do for you? There isn't anything wrong, is there?"

"No, Dad, there's nothing wrong. In fact, every thing is wonderful at this end, and I'm calling to see if you could possibly make the trip back here to help me celebrate. I've found the most wonderful girl, and we're going to be married on the 2nd of September. Do you think you and Mom might get back for the wedding?" Holding his breath, he waited.

"That's about two weeks from yesterday, right? I see no reason why your mother and I can't fly up there for your wedding. We've actually been talking about making the trip back for some time now, but somehow, we keep putting other things first. There's some business I want to take care of up there, so we'll just plan to stay for awhile."

"That's great, Dad. Do you want to stay at my apartment while you're in Colorado Springs, or could I make a reservation for you?"

"No, Dan, you probably have all kinds of details to work out getting ready for the big day. We'll work on our schedule and then make reservations accordingly. Is it going to be a big formal affair or will just a regular suit suffice? Where is the wedding going to be held and at what time? Do you want to e-mail us the details?"

"Yeah, I can do that. It's going to be a small private ceremony with only family and a few close friends. Tim is going to be my best man, and maybe you remember Nick Oldsberg who was in some of my college classes. He's here in Colorado Springs now and has agreed to be my groomsman."

"The name sounds familiar, but I'm afraid I can't place his face. I'm glad you keep in touch with Tim, though. I have always wished you were in Hayes so you could take over the home there."

"That reminds me, Dad. I wanted to ask if you still own Grandpa's cabin up in the mountains. I thought I might take Monica there sometime if it's still available. I think she'd really enjoy spending some time up there."

"Sure, we still own it. We haven't been up there for

ages, but I've paid a maintenance crew to watch over it, so I hope it's still standing," he laughed. "I'll check right away to see if any repairs need to be done. You think Monica might like to rough it a little, huh?"

His hearty laugh reminded Dan of the few really good times he'd shared with his dad, especially when he was a teenager. He had to chuckle as he remembered a vacation when his dad had taken him and Tim fishing at a camp in Minnesota. Mom was there, too, but she sat on the deck of the cabin enjoying the view. The three guys had been fishing in a rather small boat when his dad had hooked a fairly large bass. The fish had made one of those sudden big high jumps which had caused his dad to lose his balance and land in the lake, but he hadn't lost that fish. He'd just handed the rod to me with instructions to start reeling. The fish, of course, had taken off with the line and it took a good hour or more to pull him in. Dad had climbed back into the boat, dripping wet, but was determined to finish the job. It had really impressed both of us guys, and Mom had had a good laugh as she'd watched from the deck.

To answer his dad now, he said, "Yeah, Dad, I really think Mauni would like it. She lives on this small acreage and loves the outdoors. It would be quite different for her, but I still think she'd love the mountain adventure. How's Mom? Is she close enough I could say Hi to her before we hang up?"

Sally M. Russell

"Your mother had an upset stomach the last day on the ship yesterday, so she went up to her room right after we got home this morning. Let me see if she'll pick up the phone by her bed. Hold on just one second."

Shortly he heard, "Dan is that really you? I'm sorry I wasn't downstairs when you called. I could've gotten on an extension. How are you, Sweetheart?"

"I'm fine, Mom. It's good to hear your voice, but I'm sorry you aren't feeling well. Do you think you ate something that didn't agree with you, or was it maybe the water? Of course, it could've been just the final leg of a long journey."

"Oh, I don't know, Dan. It seems like these cruises and trips are getting harder all the time. Sometimes I wish we were back in Hayes where I could enjoy the big backyard, talk to the neighbors, or walk the streets without fear of being attacked by either a crazy lunatic who wants money for drugs or an out-of-control alligator roaming around."

He chuckled at her description of life, as she sees it, among the lunatics and scary alligators. "I called to tell you about my wedding in about two weeks, the one you'd probably thought would never happen. Dad thinks you can fly up and attend. It'll be great to see you."

"We'll be there if I have to crawl," she giggled. He then vividly remembered when he was small; she'd almost daily taken him to the yard to play. He'd loved her giggle, and she'd been so much fun until Dad had come home, and then she'd quickly sent him back to Nanny.

"I'm looking forward to seeing you, but I'd better let you rest now so you can feel a lot better in the morning. You know I want you feeling great when you meet my soon-to-be wife. I'm sure you'll love her *almost* as much as I do. Bye for now, Mom, I love you."

"Goodbye, Son. I can hardly wait for this wonderful event."

"Me neither. These next two weeks will probably seem like forever."

What just happened there? Both of my parents seemed pleased to hear from me. Are they mellowing as they age, or could they finally be realizing just what they've missed by not being a family with me? This call did cause me to recall some great times I had with them that I'd forgotten over the years. I wish there had been more, but I need to remember the good ones and try to forget all my disappointments. At least it sounds like they'll be at my wedding, so I guess a miracle can still happen. Thank you, God. It would be wonderful to have my father and mother really involved in my life. My children, hopefully I'll have some, could then have two sets of loving grandparents to give them love and guidance. But, right now, I'll just be happy that they're willing to come to my wedding.

CHAPTER TWENTY-TWO

While Dan was driving to the farm Sunday morning to attend church with Monica again, his thoughts were jumping from one subject to another. He has really liked Pastor Haskell's sermons and is looking forward to becoming a member after he and Monica return from their honeymoon. That reminds him that he hasn't mentioned to Monica, as yet, his plans for their trip. He's still debating whether to keep it a surprise or make sure she'd like it. "I'll have to decide soon," he mutters to himself as he turns into the drive.

When he walks in the door and sees the little guilty look on her face, he immediately knows something is up. *What has she done now? I'm beginning to think my life with this woman is going to be a constant surprise.* "What's up, Mauni? That look on your face gives you away every time, so out with it."

"It's nothing bad, Dan, but I do need to ask a big

favor from you. I know our wedding is a private ceremony and dinner, but I was telling Trudy and Ann the details of shopping for the dresses and the flowers, and....well.... Dan, Sweetheart, Honey,.....uh."

Dan held u p his hand for silence, but he couldn't quite keep a straight face. "Just cut all this cute mushy stuff, Monica, and tell me what you did. Please don't tell me we're going to have twenty more guests to provide a dinner for when you get through inviting everyone who looks at you with their sad pleading eyes." Taking her by the shoulders, he laughingly coaxed, "Come on, tell me exactly what you did so I can agree with you or plan to lock you up for the next twelve days."

"I haven't done anything yet, Dan, because I told them I would have to check with you, but Trudy and Ann both work days on September 2, and they just wondered if they and their husbands could possibly attend the wedding. They just want to see us get married, and they don't expect anything else. I told them about the announcement in the church bulletin. They had a good laugh, by the way, but they understand how church members are and hope it'll discourage any from just dropping in." She looked at him pleadingly with those beautiful blue alluring eyes that get to him every time, so what could he do?

"Monica, I don't know what I'm going to do with you. You are so kind-hearted; you'd probably take out another loan on the farm just to please everyone. By the way, have you, or are you still planning to ask Dr. Moore?"

"I did ask her, but she and her family are going to be on vacation that week."

"Well, since I have to work with those two nurses every day, I'd better agree to them and their husbands coming to the wedding. I just imagine, if I didn't, I could be in trouble big time," he grinned as he took her in his arms for a hug. "In fact, why don't you invite them to the dinner because I also have a confession to make? I just happened to see Liz Becker in a patient's room Friday and I impulsively asked if she thought it'd be possible for her and Josh to attend the wedding *and* reception. Is that my compensation for agreeing to this last request of yours?"

"You are such a big swindler, Dan Wilder, waiting for just the right moment to drop that bit of news on me, but I'm so glad you did that. They are such a darling couple, I sure hope they'll have a future together some day. I think I heard that she'll only be a sophomore in high school this year, so they have a tough road ahead of them."

"From what I observed, I'd still put my money on a very happy ending. However, she wasn't too optimistic about the wedding. Josh will be returning to college shortly, and it'd be a pretty long drive for a Friday night wedding requiring him to miss several classes so soon after the term started. She did ask if perhaps her dad and she could attend the wedding. She said she wants to get all the ideas she can for when she gets married. I told her that whatever she could work out would be fine with us. I'll still let you add your four, though."

Later, at the church, they saw the pastor for a few minutes after the service to finally complete the details for the wedding. Dan also made sure the invitation to the dinner had been extended to him and his wife. After enjoying lunch at a nearby restaurant, Dan decided he'd better get home because he was actually on call from 4 to 12 today and Monica was to work the 3 to 11 shift before having 2 days off.

On Monday and Tuesday, Monica tried to concentrate on the final plans for taking care of things while they were away. Dan hadn't mentioned where he was taking her, but he had, with that cute grin on his face, told her she would need both dressy and casual clothes.

She had been talking to her mother almost every day, but out of the blue on Monday, her mother had asked, "Monica, would you like for Keith and me to stay at the farm and look after the horses and the house while you and Dan are away?" It had caught her off guard, but when she asked about her mother's work, she'd casually informed her, "I'm retiring very soon now and moving in with Keith. I've already turned in my resignation."

"Can we meet for lunch tomorrow, Mom, so I can

get all the details on this? I have a couple of things to get done today, but I need to do some shopping and tomorrow would be great. I not only have to get some special clothes, but I haven't bought Dan's ring yet."

Her thoughts drifted back to when she'd asked for his ring size, which, of course, he didn't know. He'd then slipped his high school class ring off his finger and had a good laugh when he'd realized how many years he'd been wearing it. She quickly returned to the present when she heard her mother speaking.

"That would be great, Monica. I could take the afternoon off and go shopping with you, if you'd like me to, but I don't want to intrude."

"Oh, Mom, I'd love for you to go shopping with me. Can I pick you up about 11:30?"

"See you then, Sweetheart."

Dan's phone was ringing Wednesday afternoon when he got home from the hospital. He was expecting Monica to drop by after her shift was over, so he hoped she wasn't going to cancel their dinner together again. He was beginning to wish he'd insisted on eloping, as the time they could see each other had become less and less. "Hello," he answered, "this had better not be bad news, or I'm going to kidnap you and elope yet."

"Trouble with the wedding plans?" he heard his

father's chuckle. "Everything will work out fine, Son, just hang in there."

"Hi, Dad, I thought it was Monica calling to tell me she couldn't come over after her shift is done at 3 o'clock. It's been almost impossible to spend any quality time with her the last two weeks. Is everything all right with you and Mom?"

"We're just fine and your mother is happier than I've seen her in two years. I wanted to call and let you know that she was ready to head home right after you called so we packed and arrived about noon today. We decided we'd need the car while we're here so we drove instead of fighting all the complicated flying schedules, and we've also made reservations in Colorado Springs for next Wednesday through Saturday.

You didn't mention a rehearsal so your mom came up with this. We were wondering if we could take you and Monica, plus her mother and Keith, to dinner Thursday night. We'd love to meet them before the wedding, if that's possible. Do you think the restaurant, where the wedding dinner is going to be, could accommodate the six of us that night? Also, Dan, could just the two of us meet for lunch on Wednesday? I have a couple of things I'd really like to discuss with you."

"As long as it's not about the birds and the bees, it's a date." He couldn't keep from chuckling at his dad's thunderous laugh to that remark. "Why don't you drop by the hospital about 11:00? I'm usually through with all the surgeries I have by then, and my other regular appointments usually don't start until 1 o'clock or later. Will that give you enough time for what you want to talk to me about? As for the Thursday night dinner, that sounds great. I'll have Monica check with her mother, and I'll make a reservation for about 7:15. How does that sound?"

"That'll work out just fine, Dan. I have some business to get done here in Hayes this week, and your mom wants to go to church here on Sunday. I'm just beginning to realize how much she has missed our home here, plus her friends and the safe little town. I had been thinking about putting the house and acreage up for sale, but I'm wondering now if we should move back and just go south during the winter months.

Anyway, I'll get the business taken care of and then we'll drive up next Wednesday morning so I can meet you for lunch. I'm sure looking forward to seeing you, Son. I really mean that." Dan thought he heard his dad choke up a little, which was a surprise, but before he could reply, he heard the phone click off.

Timing had been perfect, as Monica came in the door just after he'd hung up, and he greeted her with a big hug and kiss. She was glowing, and excitedly told him about her shopping spree with her mother yesterday, and the offer about taking care of the horses. "I'd just assumed that Charlotte and Clint would have to come over every day to do the chores, but Mom says she and Keith will stay there while we're gone and watch the house and the horses. Isn't that something? Keith is still practicing law, but I know he has cut back a lot on his clients so his days aren't so long, and Mom has turned in her resignation."

"More and more I realize how God has had a hand in this from the very beginning. Nothing could have run so smoothly without His help all along the way." He picked her up and swung her around, much like Drew had done, but then he proceeded to kiss her which provided proof he definitely was <u>not</u> Drew.

While Monica was changing from her nurse's uniform into some wild plaid shorts and a green tank top, Dan had gone to the Deli to get something for them to eat. *He is so good at selecting food for the hot weather,* she mused, as they devoured their tuna salad croissant sandwiches, Cole slaw, and a piece of cherry pie, which they'd divided.

As they were eating, he told her about his father's call. She was elated, and as soon as they were finished, she went to the phone to call her mother and tell her about the Thursday night invitation to dinner. "Oh, Monica, that is so nice of them. I only wish I had thought of something like that. Keith and I will definitely plan on being there."

After they had cleared the table, they sat out on the deck for awhile and he held her snuggled in his arms with her back against his chest. "This is what I'm looking forward to; holding you just like this each and every night, and I can hardly believe it's only nine days away. But, Mauni, I've made some tentative plans for our honeymoon. I had thought about keeping them a secret, but I think I should let you decide if you'll be happy with them. Will you be honest and tell me if you'd rather go someplace else?"

"Of course, if that's what you'd like. I'll be happy anywhere, though, as long as I'm with you."

"Have you been to Chicago?" he asked and anxiously waited for her answer.

"Oh, Dan, I've wanted to go to Chicago all my life, but Dad never seemed to have the time to take us anywhere, and then Terry and I were so involved with getting the farm fixed up, we didn't go too far away from home either. Yes, I'd love to go to Chicago. I've read a lot about the things to see and do there." She turned just a little so her arms could reach up around his neck. She gently pulled his head down to her face so she could give him a sweet gentle kiss on the cheek.

"I thought we could fly into Chicago for three or

four days, or more if you'd like, and then fly back to the airport, get the car and drive to the family cabin up in the mountains. I asked Dad if he still had it, and he assured me that he has had a maintenance crew looking after it although he and Mom haven't been up there for quite a while. If it's not in very good shape, then we'll find some other place to stay. Are you game for that adventure?"

"It sounds fantastic, and I can hardly wait. Why can't the days go by a little faster so we can be on our way as husband and wife?"

"We could still take off and elope," he chuckled and then yelped as she gave him a little punch in the ribs.

"I've got to get home and feed the horses," she said as she tried in vain to get out of his arms. "Let me go, you big bear, or I'll tell Rascal and Tumbleweed it was all your fault that they about starved."

"Could we go for a little ride if I followed you home?" he asked pleadingly. "I have an early surgery again tomorrow so I won't stay after the ride."

"Let's scoot then," she said as she again tried to extricate herself from his embrace, but he pulled her back and kissed her one more time before he would let her go.

CHAPTER TWENTY-THREE

Just five more days of work, Monica thought to herself as she awoke early Thursday morning and headed to the barn. She couldn't seem to stop talking to the horses as she fed them and mucked the stalls. "Monday will actually be my last day of work because I'm doing a make-up day for when I went shopping with Charlotte and Prudence. Then I'm entitled to two days off, which will be Tuesday and Wednesday. September 1st is Thursday and my wedding is Friday, and then I'll get to be home with you two again. Well, actually after the honeymoon. Hopefully I'll be presenting you with a little one soon to love and carry on your backs. I know you'll be very careful with him or her and be another protector of a precious gift from God. I'm so happy, Rascal," she said as she patted him and gave him a hug. A soft whinny, of course, came from Tumbleweed to let her know that he wanted a hug, too. With a chuckle, she gave him a hug, patted them both, and headed to the house to dress for work.

Dan had been called to the hospital about 4 o'clock this morning, and it had been a long and tricky by-pass surgery. They'd almost lost the patient a couple of times during the five hours of stress, but it was finally over and Dan was exhausted. He'd actually had another surgery scheduled this morning at 7 o'clock, but that had been put on hold due to this other emergency. He'll now take an hour to relax and get something to eat, after he talks to the family that has been waiting for those five long hours. He'll then perform the other surgery, a hysterectomy, which, of course, made him think of Monica who will be facing the same thing in just a few short years. With all his heart, he hopes they can have at least two babies before her surgery is a necessity.

He closed his eyes for a minute and tried to imagine Monica holding their precious child, but it was he who was beaming as he held the tiny bundle of blue. "Oops, it might be pink," he said aloud. He was smiling as he made his way to the waiting room. It was quite a pleasure to reassure an anxious family that their loved one had made it through the surgery, but he also cautioned that the next 24 to 48 hours were critical.

As the days passed, Dan got in touch with all the guys in the wedding party. He also called Neil to see how things were going and if they were going to make it to the wedding.

"We've made one trip with Dad's pickup to take the few possessions we still have. Actually, that was mostly the baby things that the church people have bought for us lately. Susan has been planning how she'd like to rearrange the furniture in the house. She's really happy with the things that are there, but just wants to add her personal touches like pictures that are still at her parents. Thank goodness she'd hadn't brought them to the farm yet.

We do plan to come to the wedding and dinner, stay overnight in Colorado Springs, and then drive down to Hayes on Saturday. If at all possible, I'll be at the office on Monday, the 5th, and Dr. Noland seemed quite pleased with that. And, Mr. Groom-to-be, just in case you've been wondering, Susan has a cousin living there in Colorado Springs, where we'll be able to stay. She and her husband are also going to watch the baby while we're celebrating with you guys."

"We're looking forward to seeing you both again and wish it were an occasion where we could play with that baby. My dad may be moving back to Hayes, though, so we'll try to get down there, after you're settled, and help spoil him. Just be careful on those highways."

Friday afternoon, Dan had appointments that lasted until 4 o'clock. He went to his apartment to clean up before he drove to the farm. "I hope Mauni is home and maybe I can get her to go on a date with me. Not too many chances left to have a pre-wedding date with my fiancé'." He found her on her hands and knees in one of the flower gardens, and she was about to decline his invitation when she saw desperation on his face and couldn't refuse. She went to get cleaned up while he headed to the barn to talk to the horses, which he'd become so fond of doing. He really thought they were getting to know him and he loved to watch as they seemed to be listening to every word he said. He also loved touching them and now he knew how to get a special nudge, a whinny, or a pumping of their heads.

He and Monica went to the same restaurant close by that now has live music every Friday night. He enjoyed the chance to hold her close and also to dance a few fast numbers.

His mind, however, kept thinking about a week from tonight when she would be his wife and he wouldn't have to say goodnight or sleep alone. They returned to her house and went over the details of the wedding once again to make sure they hadn't forgotten anything. He didn't stay very late because he knew she had to work the next three days.

He went to church alone on Sunday because he wanted to make real sure that day's bulletin contained the announcement about the private wedding and dinner. After he'd sat down beside her, Charlotte grinned as she pointed to it and whispered, "That should do it."

Monday, Monica's last day of work, was a tear jerker. She had become so fond of the crew of nurses, and even the night crew had all waited to wish her well before they'd left this morning. Near the end of their shift, Trudy had slipped away for just a few minutes and then returned carrying a fairly large package, beautifully wrapped. It was almost 3 o'clock so the afternoon shift had arrived and all gathered around. With tears in her eyes, Trudy handed the package to Monica, saying, "We're all going to miss you, Monica, but we're all so happy that you're getting the chance to possibly have the family you want so badly. We'll all be praying for you, and we hope you'll come see us when you have some extra time."

"Oh, I'm planning to do that when I come to visit the lonely patients like Liz Becker does. Dan thinks that will be a wonderful way for me to keep in touch with things here and to also watch him with eagle eyes," she laughed. "Do you want me to open this before I leave or could Dan and I open it later tonight?" She'd glanced at the card and knew it was from the crew of all three shifts. She continued, "It's our very first gift and it's so thoughtful of all of you. It's so heavy I have no idea what it could be."

"You take it and open it with Dan," Trudy remarked and all the others agreed. "Each of us wish you and that handsome, no longer available, Dr. Wilder the true happiness of a lifetime, and pray that very soon a tiny little blessing from God will also come to stay."

She hugged each one there and asked if they would convey her sincere thanks to the others. Dan was planning to come out tonight so she hurried home to place their first gift on the coffee table before he got there. She then checked the country-style pork ribs she'd put in the slow cooker this morning, and covered them now with her special sauce. They were fine so she dashed to the barn for a few minutes and then put the potatoes and fresh green beans on to cook that she had washed and gotten ready last night.

When Dan wasn't there by 5:30, she became concerned and called the hospital to see if he had been called for an emergency. Sure enough, he was in OR with an accident victim, and they weren't sure how long he would be as there had been internal injuries. The patient had been brought in around 3:30, they had told her, so she realized it was about the time she was driving home.

She thanked them and had just settled down on the couch when she heard a rumble, like a truck, coming down the road. She felt vulnerable because very rarely did anyone come down her road with it ending at the dead end not far past her driveway. Her land extends to the south a little ways, where the greenhouses were to be, but also north and west where the grove of trees and riding trails are located. She went to lock the door because she couldn't see what it was, but soon watched as a UPS delivery truck pulled just past her drive and then backed in and stopped. *I haven't ordered anything lately so what in the world could he be bringing?* She watched from the sun porch as the man struggled to remove a good-sized box from the truck. She got so curious that she almost went out to help him carry it to the door.

"I'll put it wherever you like, Ma'am, because it's too heavy for a person your size to try to move it by yourself," the delivery man said as she opened the door for him.

She decided to be cautious so had him leave it right there in the sun porch. She knew she should be able to trust delivery drivers, but she didn't want to take any chances since it was after 6 o'clock now. Dan had warned her repeatedly about living out here alone so she had been trying to be very careful. A receipt had to be signed and then he was gone, but she bolted the door again before she returned to the couch. *I just wish Dan were here, but he won't always be here after we're married either. Actually, I've lived here now for almost two years by myself and have always felt safe, so why should I be afraid tonight? I don't think I'm afraid; I'm just wishing Dan were here since I've gotten used to him being around.*

It was after 6:30 when the phone rang and she was happy to hear Dan's voice. "I'm so sorry, Darling, but we just finished patching up an accident victim, and I didn't have a chance to even call you. Do you still want me to come out or should I just go on home?"

"I want you to come, but only if you're not too tired. I called the hospital about 5:30 so I knew you were in OR because of an accident. We received two wedding presents and I know I won't be able to sleep until I know what's in them. Supper's in the slow cooker and won't be done until 7 o'clock, so if you can safely drive out here, I'll feed you and then we'll see what the boxes contain."

"I was hoping you'd say that because I'm on my way and will be there in about ten more minutes. Will you let me take a little nap before I have to drive back?"

"After we eat and open the presents, you can sleep all night if you wish," she laughed, "so I'll see you soon."

Dan let out a whistle when she unlocked the door and he saw the large box. He took time, of course, to hug and kiss her affectionately. "What do you suppose that is, Sweetheart, and do you know who sent it?"

She looked sheepishly as she said, "I was sort of worried when the delivery was made as late as it was, so I just locked the door and forgot to look." She went to the box and saw that the return address was her brother's. "What in the world did they buy for us, and why did he have it delivered when they could have brought it Friday?"

"Look at the size of that box, Mauni. They couldn't get that in their car unless they have a van as well as the little car they drove down for the cookout."

"You're right, as usual, Dr. Wilder," and she gave him a rather hard slap on the arm.

"Oh, I'm sorry, Dan. I didn't mean to hit you that hard," she apologized as she grinned and rubbed his arm affectionately. "Shall we eat first, since it's almost 7 o'clock? I can imagine your stomach is talking to you pretty good by now, and I'm getting rather hungry myself."

As he rubbed his arm and moaned, as if he had been terribly wounded, he headed for the kitchen and the wonderful smell of barbeque.

When they were finished, Monica grabbed a sharp knife and they both headed for the big box on the sun porch. When they'd finally succeeded getting out all of the packing, they found a beautiful walnut table, about 20" in diameter, with the most exquisite carvings. They just looked at each other, neither of them finding words to express their feelings.

"We have one more present," she said as she grabbed his hand and pulled him toward the living room and the other beautifully wrapped gift. "This is so exciting," she said as they sat on the couch and studied the size of this box. She had him lift it just to see how heavy it was. "Can you even imagine what it could be?"

"Well, it's not another table," Dan almost whispered as he appeared so touched by this generosity. "Those nurses wouldn't give us a bomb, would they, because I took you away from them?"

"If that were the case, it'd be more aimed at me for taking *you* away from them, not at you for taking *me* away from them. Let's forget about that possibility, though, and you can help me take the ribbon and wrapping off. We have to do it very carefully, though," she instructed him. "I need to save them as brides are supposed to do." When the paper had been removed, they saw that the box was from one of the best jewelry and gift shops in the city, and inside they found a lovely pewter candle stand holding a large 10" vanilla candle and a note which read:

We checked with Pastor Haskell to be sure you were going to light the Keepsake unity candle during the ceremony on Friday evening. Our hope is that you will use this candle and its stand at that time so you may always have it in your home as a true Keepsake. Each time you light it, may you believe even more the unity God has brought into your lives.

Our Best Wishes and
May God Bless You Both
The Nurses on Fourth Floor

As tears ran down her cheeks, Monica couldn't take her eyes off the candle and its most beautiful stand. "I'll talk to Pastor Haskell tomorrow and tell him that we have been given this and I'll bring it to the church on Friday afternoon. When we bring it home, we'll use the table from Drew to display it. They'll both be beautiful keepsakes for us to enjoy."

"They will certainly be a wonderful addition to our home, wherever that may be as the years go by," he added.

When he saw her turning toward him, with a little frown on her face, he just smiled as he attempted to rub the frown marks away. He then remarked, "With all the babies you are planning to have, after you become Mrs. Daniel Wilder, we may need to get a larger home. Wouldn't you agree?" He was chuckling as he took her in his arms and proceeded to give her one of their special affectionate kisses.

"Are you going to hold my head while I take a little nap, Mauni, or do you have other things you need to get done? I can't stay too long because I never know when I'll get called again. The other doctors are taking some days off so they can fill in for me while you and I are gone, so this week hasn't been the easiest when all I can think about is our wedding."

"I'll be happy to hold your head, Dan, unless you'd be more comfortable on the bed."

"Would you be on the bed with me?" he asked as he nuzzled her neck and earlobe.

"No, I'm going to be sure we're married before I let you talk me into that, but I sure am looking forward to it," she giggled.

"You drive a hard bargain, Sweetheart," he whispered as he turned so he could lay his head on her lap. Surprisingly, he was soon fast asleep.

CHAPTER TWENTY-FOUR

Dan's father was there Wednesday when Dan and another doctor came out of the OR unit. Dan invited him to come meet his dad. As they approached the tall, very distinguished looking man waiting for them with a big smile on his face, he said, "Dad, I'd like you to meet one of the other surgeons here at the hospital, Dr. Stephen Myers. Steve, this is my dad, Dr. Paul Wilder. He was a dentist for quite a few years down in Hayes before retiring about three years ago. The two men shook hands, and then Steve excused himself and headed down the corridor toward his office. "So, are you ready for some lunch?" Dan asked.

"Since it would be around 1 o'clock in Florida, my stomach is talking to me a little bit," his dad chuckled, "although I've had a few days to get adjusted to Colorado time again. Is there a restaurant close by that is a little on the quiet side so we can talk?"

"There's a real nice restaurant about a block or so down the street. Would you like to walk, or should I get my car?"

"That's up to you, Dan. I'd love to walk, but do you have the time to walk and still get back in time for your appointments?"

"I set my first appointment this afternoon at 2:00 which should give us enough time to do the walk and the talk," he laughed.

"Well, I hardly know where to begin, Son, because I have so much to apologize for. I know I wasn't the father I should have been to you, but I was so in love with your mother that I didn't want to share her with anyone. I didn't think I wanted children, so when she told me she was going to have a baby, I threw a fit and told her I'd have nothing to do with it.

You see, I grew up in Pueblo where my dad taught at the college. I'd just had the one younger brother, Clifford, and I'd always felt that my dad and mom loved him a lot more than they did me. It seemed as if they always blamed me for whatever went wrong and put a lot of other responsibilities on my shoulders, too. I'd grown up feeling I was always alone, but it never occurred to me that I was causing you to feel the same way by my actions. I'd decided at a pretty young age that when I got married, my wife was going to spend her time with me when I was home. I'd worked every summer for my grandpa on the farm, just a little way outside of town, saving for my college tuition, while Clifford got to go to the Church camps, take trips with other families, and spend a lot of time at the city pool."

They had reached the restaurant, quickly placed their order, and he continued. "I met your mother in college, and for some reason, she fell in love with me, and I was in my glory. Her father, Grandpa Colman, was one great man, and when he learned we were serious and wanted to get married, he actually paid my tuition so I could finish dental school sooner. One of the conditions, however, was that I would have my practice in Hayes.

And that's not all of it, Dan. Your inheritance from his estate paid for *your* medical training, also. Even though you were not yet twelve years old, you had apparently talked to him a lot about wanting to be a surgeon when you grew up. He asked me to handle the trust money, but not to be too strict with the purse strings whatever you finally decided to do.

I wanted you to learn financial responsibility, as well as all the medical techniques you would need to become a surgeon. When you decided that was what you really wanted to do, I tried to be as generous as I thought Grandpa would've wanted, but you were quite the conservative one. The remainder of his estate, including the cabin you asked about, is also yours. He instructed me to give it all to you when I thought you would need it most, but no later than your 35th birthday."

Reaching into his briefcase, he pulled out an envelope containing a deed which had been transferred to Daniel Duane Wilder. "I have used the inheritance money, as needed, to maintain the cabin over the years. I remembered how much you enjoyed going up there with your grandpa, and thought you might like to own it someday, but there is still quite a bit left of your inheritance for you to do with as you wish. Of course, it's also accumulated quite a bit of interest over the years. I'm really sorry he passed away when you were only twelve, but I'm sure you remember the good times you shared." He then pulled another envelope out of the briefcase and handed it to Dan.

After glancing at it for a second, Dan just stared at his dad. "You've got to be kidding, Dad. You mean to tell me I went through all my medical training, you maintained the cabin, and this is still left. Quite a tidy sum, I must say. If I had known, I could've had a high old time in college," he said, laughing, "but I'm so glad you held on to it for me because I have a much greater use for it now than during my schooling. Gosh, Dad, I don't know what to say. Are you sure you and Mom don't need some of this?"

"No, Dan, we don't need any of that, and Daniel

Colman helped take care of that also before he made these provisions for you. Before he died in 1984, I was well established in my dental practice, you were his only grandchild, since your mother was also an only child, and his wife, your grandmother, had died of cancer a few months earlier. After sitting beside her bed for almost a year, his heart just gave up when she was gone, but he definitely had his papers in order. He was a financial wizard, loved investing in real estate, as well as doubling the assets of the bank he'd inherited from his father and grandfather. Actually, Dan, your great, great grandfather was in the original group that came from New York. He opened the first bank in Hayes, which was financed partly by who else but Jeremiah Hayes. In just a few years, though, it was completely solvent and Jeremiah Hayes had made a considerable profit. It is now owned by a group of local men, headed by Noah Hayes. That was one of the last things Daniel Colman accomplished before his death."

"I certainly do remember the times I spent with Grandpa Colman, but what about your folks? Was I too young to know them, or were you estranged from them?"

"No, I had made peace with them and myself, thank goodness. My folks were killed in a fire that destroyed my grandfather's farmhouse. Dad and Mom moved into it after both my grandparents had died. Cliff had gone into the ministry so we were both on our own, and Dad decided to try his hand at some farming after he'd retired from teaching. No one seemed to know for sure just what had happened, but it was assumed the furnace had malfunctioned during the night. That was shortly after you were born, and they did get to see their firstborn grandchild."

The two had taken time to eat their lunches, but Dan was so interested in what his dad was telling him, the time had really slipped away. When he finally glanced at his watch, he was really amazed. "Gosh, Dad, my patient is going to wonder what happened to me. I didn't realize we'd been talking for so long, but it's almost 2 o'clock and I have to get to the office. Would you and Mom want to ride out to the farm with me this evening and meet Monica, or would you rather wait until tomorrow night?"

"With the allergies I somehow developed to animals in college, Dan, I'd better pass on that. I don't want to take any chances of having to miss your wedding. I think that's just one more thing I deprived you of. I certainly did understand how much you wanted a horse or a pet, but I couldn't tolerate being around any animal, and I had to protect myself so I could handle my dental practice. I couldn't bring myself to admit to my son that I had this deficiency so I again failed to establish a rapport with you. You run along now, I'll get the check, and I hope we'll be able to talk a lot more in the years to come."

"See you tomorrow, Dad, and thanks so much for all this information."

As Dan jogged back to the hospital, his mind was full of all he had learned in two or three hours. He'd always known that he had a deep rooted love for his family, but he had almost given up hope of ever being able to express it. To hear the real story now about why his dad had acted as he had, and to realize that Grandpa Colman had paid his way through all those years of medical school, internship, and residence, it was almost too much for him to comprehend.

I wonder how Monica will feel when I present my gift to her tonight. Will she finally realize just how much I love her? It's a drop in a bucket compared to what I've just been handed, but this is just the beginning of my plans for her and our future together. He wasn't even trying to keep the smile off his face as he arrived at his office, but it grew even larger when he saw his patient just checking in.

CHAPTER TWENTY-FIVE

Over the last couple of weeks, Dan had taken the time to tell all his regular patients about his upcoming marriage and that he would be gone for at least two weeks. He had also told them, if necessary, how to contact his replacement. Everything had gone fine until the last appointment Wednesday afternoon when Patrick Downard, about 40 years old, came in moaning and in tears as he was holding his side and back. Dan had wanted to do the surgery about six weeks ago, a fairly routine outpatient procedure for a gallbladder problem, but the patient had insisted it wasn't his gallbladder and had walked out of the office. Now, of all times, he's going to be forced to have it done.

"Patrick," Dan said, "I can refer you to Dr. Myers, who will take very good care of you, but my schedule just won't allow me to do it for over two weeks, and you need it done now before you really get into trouble."

"You're doing this because I wouldn't believe your

diagnosis before, aren't you? I heard doctors were supposed to be compassionate and not hold a grudge. I don't want any other doctor operating on me, so I'll just suffer until you change your mind." Tears were welling up in his eyes as he tried to stand up, but then he slowly sank back into the chair in pain."

Dan picked up the phone and ordered a gurney, stat. "Is your wife here with you or should I call her?"

"Oh, . . .wife. . .in waiting. . .room," he muttered as he doubled over and sobbed, "so sorry. . .for what. . .I said."

"I'll get a consent form brought in for you to sign and you'll be on your way to the operating room. I'll have to determine if we can still do the outpatient procedure, but we'll get you relief from that pain."

Dan then called the front desk, asked to have Mrs. Downard brought back, as well as a consent form, ASAP.

The gurney had gotten there and they had the patient strapped on when his wife and the nurse arrived with the form to sign. After explaining the situation to Mrs. Downard, he told her how to get to the waiting room, located just outside the OR unit, and that he would talk to her when the procedure was finished.

He went back inside his office and called Monica, who, of course, understood that he couldn't walk away from a person in pain. Their plans would, of course, depend on how the surgery went. It was only 4 o'clock, so with any luck, they would still have a few hours to be alone together for maybe the last time before the wedding.

After the examination and an x-ray, Dan decided he could still try the non-invasive procedure first, although the stones were where they were causing the most pain. Everything went well in the operating room, and they were finished by a little after 6 o'clock. Since the patient had been rather upset and it was later in the day than Dan usually performed surgery, he'd elected to admit him overnight just to be sure he was going to be all right. He visited a few minutes with his wife, and she also agreed that staying at the hospital overnight would probably be best.

After leaving instructions for Dr. Myers, Dan quickly showered and donned the clean clothes he'd brought this morning because of the plans for this evening. He was soon on his way to Monica's because he was definitely on a mission tonight, and he didn't want to put it off any longer. He patted his shirt pocket, glanced at the manila envelope he'd placed on the seat beside him and smiled. He hoped she would be happy with his surprise gift, and also all the information he'd received from his dad.

꙳

When Monica had gotten her mail today, her bank statement had come. While she was waiting for Dan, she decided she might as well check it, but became concerned when she realized her mortgage check had not been cancelled. She was sure it had been written, but checked the register again to confirm it. Everything else checked out fine, so she would call in the morning to make sure it had been received. She certainly didn't want to leave on her honeymoon with the mortgage not paid. She then heard Dan's car, which she had learned to recognize, so laid the statement aside and ran to the sun porch to unlock the door for him.

He lifted her up into the air and twirled her around as he sang some made-up words about "a surprise there is going to be, when I give her a gift to see, and then I will tell her, all that does matter, is that my love so true will never make her feel blue."

"Put me down, Dan, but what was that little ditty all about? Do you have a surprise for me tonight?" She fluttered her eyelashes and smiled. "First, though, you haven't eaten yet, have you? Just put me down and let me get you some food, and then we can talk."

"I don't know if I can eat until after I give you my surprise and then tell you about my meeting with Dad. You'll never believe, Mauni, all that I learned during that lunch! It may take a while, though, so maybe I'd better eat a little something so I don't collapse during my very long and exciting story." His face was glowing with excitement, and he had her tingling all over as she fixed him a plate of food and both of them a glass of lemonade.

After he'd finished eating, he grabbed her hand and pulled her into the living room and onto the couch. "I have something for you, Darling, that I hope will convince you just how much I love you. It's my wedding gift to you, and though it isn't sparkling like a true diamond, or precious like an heirloom, the gift I'm giving you tonight will give you security that no gem or any piece of art could. So, please close your eyes."

"Dan, what are you going to do?"

"Just close your eyes and you'll know very soon."

Monica closed her eyes, but oh how she wanted to peek. He lifted her hand and with the palm up, she felt him place something on it--a piece of paper--what in the world?

"You may open your eyes now, Sweetheart," and as she looked into those beautiful eyes, she could see the anticipation dancing in them. She then glanced down at the folded paper in her hand that had notary stamps and signatures all over it. She started to ask, but then realized what she was holding, and she could only stare at him. "Dan, you didn't!"

"Yes, Darling, I did. Your mortgage is paid in full so the farm and house are both yours free of debt."

"But,. . .But," She couldn't think of anything to say so

she just kissed him. "I got my bank statement today and I wondered why my check hadn't been cancelled."

"Oh, that." He reached into his pocket and pulled out her check and handed it to her. "They gave that back to me after I had negotiated the settlement. I may have to make a deal with you after we're married, however, because I think I'll need some land to build a larger home for all those babies you're going to have."

She smiled as if she were imagining the possibility of having a houseful of little ones with all the laughter, singing, playing and praying that goes into making a house a home.

Dan pulled her into his arms and, as they cuddled, he told her about the meeting with his dad and all the facts and figures that he had absorbed. She was as amazed as he'd been, but they were both so thankful to God. Together they made a promise to always be good stewards of His gifts.

CHAPTER TWENTY-SIX

Thursday went by quickly as Dr. Myers accompanied Dan on his rounds so he would be familiar with any patients Dan was leaving in his care. The heart patient was, of course, the most critical, but he's improving daily. Dr. Myers had been in the operating room during the whole procedure and knows the steps to be taken. Most of the patients had been released, but three would still be there for another day or two. Dan said his goodbyes to the staff about 11:30 and headed to his apartment to finish packing. Then, after getting ready for the dinner that his dad and mom are hosting tonight, he went and rehearsed for the ceremony tomorrow night. He just couldn't stop thinking, however, about the magnificent gift he'd received for his wedding--his parents are here and want to be a part of his life.

It turned out to be a great evening, and Dan knew that his dad was truly smitten when Monica, without a moment's hesitation, had given him a big hug and kiss on the cheek when they'd been introduced. His mother had been all smiles, as well, as they had embraced. The weather was still quite warm and Monica had worn a cute sky blue sundress with a border of white flowers around the hem and white dangling earrings. With her dark hair and blue eyes, she was a knockout.

Of course, Mona, Keith, Elaine and Paul got along well and the conversation never hit a snag. When they'd parted, they were all looking forward to seeing each other tomorrow night at the big event.

He'd been told he couldn't see Monica tomorrow until the ceremony, so Dan asked if he could drive her home tonight since she'd come with her mom and Keith. "It'll save you a trip," he reminded them. They decided he could if he would leave before midnight. "I never get to stay after midnight," he chuckled, "so I get a chance to really kiss her goodnight?"

"I guess Monica is old enough to make her own decisions, Dan, so we'll trust the two of you to do the right thing," Mona replied, "but you'd better not have dark circles under your eyes at your wedding tomorrow night," she added with a giggle.

∽

Friday night finally arrived, and the yellow mums, lush greenery and baby's breath, entwined in the two large tapered candelabra at the front of the church made a lovely floral background, and the candles, giving off a soft glow, gave the altar area a magically touched aura. The florist had added a little more loveliness by fastening big ivory bows at the ends of the first five pews, and greenery with ivory button mums surrounded their unity candle.

She'd presented yellow rose corsages to the three mothers and Diane, Drew's wife, and then the yellow rose boutonnieres to Paul, Keith, and Claude, plus Clint and Derrick, who are serving as ushers. She then located Drew, who will give the bride away, in the room with Dan, Tim, and Nick.

When she arrived at the bride's dressing room, she was really excited at the genuine beauty of the three of them. She was checking to see that all was correct and proper when at 6:50 Mona peeked in and loved what she saw. She announced that Terry's parents had been taken to their seats, they were about to seat Dan's parents and would be ready to take her and Keith and Diane down shortly. With a hug and a sincere wish, "May God give you a very long and happy marriage this time, Monica," she smiled and then slipped away.

Paul and Keith had also been with Dan, Tim, Nick and Drew for awhile listening to stories about Dan and Tim growing up in Hayes, and Nick supplying some of the wild and funny experiences of their college days.

After giving Dan a thumbs up for "Good Luck," the two men left to be seated. At 6:55, when they heard the music begin, the guys knew it was time to make their entrance. "You sure you've got the ring, Tim?" Dan asked for about the umpteenth time. Nick and Tim just ushered him to the side door of the sanctuary and then, led by the pastor, they took their places at the front of the church.

A quick knock on the door meant it was time for the procession to start, so the three best friends opened the door to find Drew standing there ready to escort his beautiful sister down the aisle. They left the room to witness the beginning of a new life for the one who had lost one love but had gained a chance to love again.

The Wedding Ceremony

Soft music was being played by a quartet of instruments, a Casio, guitar, clarinet, and pompom drum, as Prudence, and then Charlotte, walked slowly down the aisle in their knee length rust-colored silk sheath dresses. Their bouquets were small cascades of ivory button mums accented with a few deep yellow rose buds and baby's breath. The girls reached their places and then turned to watch Monica come down the aisle on the arm of her brother. She looked lovely in her filmy ivory silk dress fashioned with spaghetti straps, the fitted bodice covered in front with tiny ruffles down to the empire waist, and the skirt billowing to just below her knees. A pair of simple tear-drop pearl earrings was her only jewelry. The bridal bouquet was a large cascade of deep yellow roses surrounded with the tiny button mums and baby's breath.

When she had taken just a few steps, she heard the most beautiful baritone voice, and she knew immediately that Dan was singing. She was spellbound.

> The first time I saw you was the moment I loved you
> Your smile was the loveliest I'd ever seen.
> I wanted to know you, and I couldn't forget you
> So I was embarrassed making a scene,
> But you were sweet and kind, and soothed my mind
> And our love just grew and grew,
> Oh, Darling, <u>How I love you!</u>
>
> And now that I've really, really gotten to know you,
> Roses are blooming whenever you're near.
> You come to me now with the freshness of springtime,
> And we'll wait for the wedding bells to hear,
> For God has given me--a love divine
> That I'll cherish for all time,
> Just because, <u>He made you mine!</u>

It was a good thing that Drew was beside her, because how she made it on down the aisle, Monica will never know. Dan is holding her arm now, and the pastor is speaking.

"We are here today to witness and celebrate the uniting of these two special people in Holy Matrimony. In my meetings with them, I have been impressed with how they are now entering into this marriage, not lightly or inadvisably, but discreetly and soberly. Marriage is an honorable estate, and I must ask if there is anyone who has reason why these two should not be joined in marriage, make it known at this time.

Who is giving Monica to be married to Daniel?

Her mother and I, her brother, Drew

Daniel Duane Wilder, do you take Monica Marie Reynolds to be your wedded wife?

Will you love her, comfort her, honor and keep her, so long as you both shall live?

I will.

Monica Marie Reynolds, will you take Daniel Duane Wilder to be your wedded husband? Will you love him, comfort him, honor and keep him, so long as you both shall live?

I will.

The song, "God By My Side" was sung by Jerry Price, who was accompanied by the instruments, and Monica's eyes filled with tears. The words had become so meaningful to her since the night Dan had given her the diamond ring and Jerry had come to their table and had sung it directly to her.

The day I saw you standing there,
I knew God was by my side,
And if my faith could be strong enough,
You would someday be my bride.

With sunlight shining in your eyes,
Or moonlight on your face,
For me to find someone as sweet as you,
I had relied upon His grace.

Not by chance or a human scheme,
Only God's hand holding fast
To His plan for you and me, My Love,
As we shared what was our past.

And now I'm thanking Him, My Dear,
As I have you at my side.
We can face the future together
With God as our perfect guide.

Yes, God will be our perfect guide.

Completing their personally written vows and enthusiastically saying the 'I do's,' they then kneel while "The Lord's Prayer" is sung by Jerry and accompanied softly by the Casio.

After the rings are described by Pastor Haskell as a symbol of an unbroken circle of love which has no beginning or end, and it should serve as a lifelong reminder of the vows taken and promises given today, they are exchanged. They each are given a candle from the candelabra and together light the unity candle as they gaze into each other's eyes. When they return to their places at the altar, Pastor Haskell then pronounces them husband and wife.

This is what Dan has been waiting for, and he takes full advantage of the opportunity to kiss his bride. Not able to keep from chuckling, Pastor Haskell says, "May I introduce the extremely happy Dr. Dan Wilder and his wife, Monica." There was an eruption of applause from the guests, as Dan, still holding Monica in a tender bear hug, looked out at everyone, grinned and whispered, "She's all mine!"

When the congratulations and best wishes had been received, Dan announced that the limousine outside, carrying the bridal party, would be the car for the others to follow if they were unsure of where the restaurant was located. Most of the bridal party had come to the church in the limousine and had left their cars at the restaurant. Only Drew and Diane had come in their own car, as they had followed Mona, Keith, and the bride. Before coming on to the restaurant, they'd again elected to stay behind to help Mona with the unity candle and the few gifts that had been dropped off by church members.

CHAPTER TWENTY-SEVEN

The tables at the restaurant, covered with white tablecloths and beautifully adorned with flowers, were set in a rectangle with seating on the outside, and a table holding the cake was in the center. It was after 11 o'clock when the fabulous meal had been finished, Dan and Monica had cut the cake and fed each other a bite, and toasted with champagne as their arms were entwined. The quartet was now playing music suitable for slow dancing. Everything was perfect, but the night was slipping away and Dan knew he and his wife had a plane to catch to Chicago. If they missed it, they would have to wait until tomorrow morning, and he had a rendezvous planned that he certainly didn't want to miss tonight.

Monica was surrounded with guests when he apologized for interrupting but said he'd like to dance with his wife. He escorted Monica onto the dance floor so he could talk to her quietly. "Honey, where is your luggage? We have to get to the airport to catch our plane, so we really need to leave pretty soon."

"Oh, I'm sorry, Dan. My luggage is in Keith's car so you'll need to get him to open the trunk for you."

"I'll get it transferred to my car, but can you be ready to go in ten or fifteen minutes?"

Snapping to attention, she smiled as she said, "At your command, Dr. Wilder, I'll be right with you." Before he realized what she was doing, Monica had kicked off her shoes and was standing on one of the chairs asking for attention.

"To all my family and friends, I want to thank you all so much for sharing with Dan and me the most wonderful event in a person's life. However, my new husband has informed me that we have a plane to catch so we need to get to the airport, pronto. We want you all to stay as long as you like, enjoy the music, the dancing, fellowship of friends, as well as more cake, coffee before you drive, or whatever else you want. We love you all, and we'll see you when we return."

Letting out a moan, Dan went to find Keith, whom he had seen dancing with Mona while he'd been talking to Monica. He'd hoped to slip away so they didn't have a line of cars following them on their way to the airport, but, apparently the guys had understood the need to reach the airport without any extra celebrations, so they had stayed in the restaurant.

They had arrived at the airport and gotten checked in with just a few minutes to spare. They'd also drawn some admiring smiles and attention since they hadn't had time or a place to change from their wedding clothes. Of course, Monica was willing to explain to anyone who showed an interest in listening.

Their suite at the tiny Raphael Hotel, off Michigan Avenue, was unique. They stayed five days and had so much fun and saw so many things that Monica was on cloud nine. The most fun, however, according to the new bride, was finding, or trying to find the cabin in the mountains.

Dan had been so sure he knew exactly where that cabin was, but after a day and a half of hunting, asking directions, and being completely frustrated, he finally called his dad on his cell phone. As Dan fumed, Monica couldn't keep from giggling as she could hear her new father-in-law's laughter clear across the car. "If you'd told me you were going up there on this trip, Dan, I would've drawn you a map." And his dad continued to chuckle.

After determining where they were now, Paul proceeded to give him directions and to laughingly tell him he hadn't done too badly as he was only about fifty miles off course.

"Thanks, Dad," Dan said rather disgustedly although he couldn't hold back a grin as he watched Monica trying to cover up her giggles with her hands. "I'm just waiting for the day when I can pay you back for laughing at my expense, though. Maybe we'll have to go on another fishing trip and if a fish doesn't pull you into the lake, maybe I'll push you in."

"I've learned my lesson about fishing from a small boat, Dan, but I'd love to take one of those Minnesota fishing trips again. Let's be sure to plan one for the four of us."

"Sounds great, but now I'm on the way to this cabin. When we get back, I'll let you know how the maintenance crew has performed over the years, and I must thank you again for giving Monica a good laugh. I may make her climb the hill up to the cabin if she doesn't straighten up." He'd finally chuckled. "Tell Mom we're fine and we'll see you soon."

"Have fun, both of you. I hope you find all the fishing equipment, tennis rackets, etc., that are supposed to be there, although you may never get around to using them on this trip," he chuckled. "Goodbye now."

Dan had called his dad close to noon on Friday so they found the cabin long before it turned dark. It was a beautiful setting and everything was in perfect shape. They'd stopped at a little grocery store and bought a few supplies. As Monica was putting them away, she realized how thrilled she was to be far from the hustle and bustle of the big city. Although she had enjoyed Chicago, she was looking forward to having her husband to herself and just relaxing for a few days in this most serene setting. She'd glanced out the wide-view window to take in the beautiful sky and scenery, but she also saw Dan dragging in the larger of her two suit-cases.

When he got inside and saw her watching him, he announced, "Mrs. Wilder, I think you have enough clothes with you for a month or more. I just wish we could stay that long, but right now my back is tired from driving for two days and dragging this luggage, and I have decided we need a nice long nap." In his best Bogart impersonation, he said, "Come with me, Sweetheart, and maybe we can practice a little more on getting our first baby on its way." He took her hand and led her into a large rustic bedroom with a four-poster bed that did look very inviting. She undressed, slipped into one of her new sexy gowns, and was the first to get under the covers, so she lay and watched as Dan struggled with the buttons of his shirt. When he'd reached the last one, she giggled and said, "Need some help there, Doc?"

He dropped the shirt on the floor, stepped out of his jeans and started toward the bed, his intentions quite clear. She was admiring this extremely masculine specimen, and it was still hard for her to believe that she was his wife. When he reached the bed, he quickly threw the covers back, and as he drank in her beauty, he whispered softly, "No more hiding, My Dear Sweet Mrs. Monica Marie Wilder, because I want to love every inch of you, and I'm so hoping there'll be no loud noises or interruptions here like there were in the big city."

Giggling, she reached out her arms, and murmured, "Well, then, Dr. Daniel Duane Wilder, why don't you come and love every inch of me?"

And he did just that as his arms enfolded his only true love.

EPILOG

Two little boys, Paul Colman, 3, and Duane Morgan, 18 months, are getting fidgety and anxious as they wait with their grandparents for their mom and dad to arrive with their new baby sister, Danielle Marie. The big brick circular drive off the dead end road, which is now blacktopped, leads to a large colonial home which was built while Monica was pregnant with little Paul. It faces toward the southwest so the tall mountains in the distance can be admired, and from the large deck in the back, you can see the grove of trees where they love to ride. They go often to enjoy the coolness of the shade and watch the small ripples on the pond. Dan really surprised Monica with a life-sized statue of a horse that he placed in the center of the circular drive, and along with bushes and flowers, it is a delight to the many friends and family who come to visit.

The yard at the farm house, kept to perfection, now includes a beautiful front yard to the south where the greenhouses had originally been planned. Mona and Keith were married the 1st of January, after Monica and Dan's wedding in September, and then they bought the house when Dan started drawing plans for their new home. Dan and Monica had decided to live in the apartment in town so they would be closer to each other when he was on duty at the hospital. Monica laughingly said it was because the bed was larger and so much more comfortable than at the farm. Even so, it took so long for the first pregnancy that Mona was beginning to wonder if she would ever be, as she calls herself, an efficient and so convenient babysitter.

Keith retired and boasts that he's in seventh heaven. He has, so far, besides designing the front entrance and yard, enlarged the barn, bought two more nice riding horses, two little Shetland ponies for the little boys, works in the yard with Mona and enjoys retirement to the fullest. They travel once or twice a year, but they really love their home and being close to their three darling grandchildren.

Danielle was the last of Dan and Monica's children, but they feel so blessed to have the three. God allowed Monica almost four and a half years of health to have the children, but during this last pregnancy, trouble had arisen. After the delivery, the necessary surgery had been performed.

Drew and Diane have also added to the grandchildren with a little boy who is now almost two. They come to visit on school breaks and, of course, during the summers.

Grandpa and Grandma Wilder have also ventured

onto once forbidden territory for Paul because of his allergies. Everyone was elated with the discovery that he is now fine at the house and also at the barn. He and Elaine often go riding and have invested in several horses that they keep on their land in Hayes where they now make their permanent home. A trail and horses are available for riding, and they have a well-trained staff to give lessons and supervise the operation. They have become an active part of the annual Fall Festival held in Hayes each September which gives more people the opportunity to ride.

Paul and Elaine are frequent visitors to Colorado Springs resulting in it becoming a very close knit family. Trips to Minnesota and the mountain cabin have been enjoyed by the entire clan, and Dan is elated that the lack of communication which had been the cause of the estrangement with his dad is no longer a problem.

ABOUT THE AUTHOR

Galesburg, Illinois was Sally's home from the age of three to sixty-seven. It wasn't a large city, and her teen years were filled with many activities at school and also at a well-chaperoned youth center close by. Her home was just a half block from a riding stable, and she was able to go riding several times before residential building caused the stable to move outside of the city limits. Her uncle also owned a farm where a few horses were kept.

She'd always felt that riding was an unforgettable experience, so she could sympathize with her character, Dr. Dan Wilder, when he couldn't, during his youth, even get near the one animal with which he was so fascinated.

Sally now lives in Lawrence, Kansas, with her husband, J.T. After spending over five years in the ever growing Charlotte, NC, she is now content to live in a somewhat smaller area again, although Lawrence is a very active college community. She's involved in the Women's Ministries at her church, and enjoys being close to family.